"I read Alan Taylor's book "MY MAI TAI." I found it exciting, humorous, and well written with good usage of the adverbial clause, which enhances the meaning and flow of his narratives. From the moment I started reading his book, I couldn't put it down. Well worth the read!!"

J. Roberts

"I read 'My Mai Tai' with great anticipation – I couldn't wait to experience the next escapade that the characters would get into. It was a humorous read during which I chuckled my way through from beginning to end. It provided me with a nostalgic vacation in which I re-called many of my own personal experiences during past vacations."

R. Black

"It's a winner! I enjoyed it immensely."

Ronnie

"This is a fun, humorous romp around the Hawaiian islands where you will meet some unforgettable characters!"

Carolyn

"The characters were terrific! They intrigued me so much and the stories were funny. I related much of this book to my own experiences as a traveler."

Joanie

"A fun book to read with crazy things happening. Very descriptive passages. I could relate to some of the stories since similar things have happened to me."

Angela

My Mai Tai

THE HAWAIIAN CONDO CAPERS

ALAN TAYLOR

Order this book online at www.trafford.com
or email orders@trafford.com

Most Trafford titles are also available at major online book retailers.

Printed in the United States of America.

ISBN: 978-1-4907-4586-2 (sc)
ISBN: 978-1-4907-4587-9 (e)

Library of Congress Control Number: 2014915914

Trafford rev. 09/04/2014

 www.trafford.com

North America & international
toll-free: 1 888 232 4444 (USA & Canada)
fax: 812 355 4082

CONTENTS

ACKNOWLEDGEMENTS

This book was based on a number of humorous experiences while vacationing in Hawaii with my wife Brenda and several close friends. I owe its existence to the experiences we jointly shared and the colorful characters we met and partied with. None of the characters in the book, however, are real people. Brenda has been particularly helpful in supporting this work and encouraging me to publish it.

The tone of my prose was inspired by the work of Carl Hiaasen and the books he wrote entitled *Bad Monkey, Paradise Screwed* and *Skinny Dip*.

PROLOGUE

*B*ud and Tina excitedly planned their annual visit to Hawaii. They could hardly wait to meet up again with their bizarre acquaintances on Kuhio Beach, among them: the Admiral, a likable rogue with a questionable past; Pam the ex-nun; Rita the barmaid and Brad the accountant from Chicago who never strayed from the bar throughout his annual three week vacation.

The story relates a series of light-hearted events most North Americans will relate to who have travelled to a vacation spot in a warm setting to escape the cold of winter. But little did the couple know that this time two new acquaintances were about to share their holiday: the mysterious Rocco with connections to the underworld and Rick the charismatic nightclub singer. There's an element of mystery surrounding Rocco – an insecure and shady *character involved in illegal activities. Bud and Tina are left at the end of the story wondering who murdered him.*

The mood of MY MAI TAI is upbeat and light-hearted. It is a story in which the reader is provided with a mini-vacation — escaping with Bud and Tina and sharing in their hilarious adventures. It is a book the reader will find hard to put down, one that will make them laugh out loud when the funny side of some seemingly ordinary situation emerges.

CHAPTER 1

Getting Ready

God is it pissin' down big time or am I dreaming I'm taking a shower? Bud queried rhetorically. Lost in thought, Bud Topper gazed absentmindedly out the window. The windswept rain and sleet beat incessantly in a tireless attempt to pierce the brittle surface of the glass. He snuggled deeply into the warmth and sanctuary of the inner recess of his overstuffed armchair, engaged in a trancelike stupor ... drifting, suspended in motion – looking but seeing nothing.

Slowly his head began a downward motion, bobbing towards a resting place on his hairy chest as he journeyed into a deep sleep.

Suddenly a rasping snore burst from his throat and with a jerk he snapped upright. A quick shake of his head brought him back to consciousness – collecting his senses enough to focus at arms length on the sight in the street below. The spectacle stared back at him with stark reality; the bleak and dreary picture was a mirror-image of his drab mood.

Work in the form of unfinished briefs and papers littered his desk – over here a written proposal that was going nowhere, over there an itemized invoice awaiting his signature. The wastebasket at his feet overflowed its contents. Scrunched up wads of scratch paper covered the floor – he was loaded with work from the office and too damn tired to do it.

"When the hell does the work end? Does it ever end? I guess not for this cowboy," he said to no one in particular.

As the scene below gained focus Bud began to make out shadowy shapes scurrying along the sidewalk; fuzzy objects blending into the grey twilight. People darted quickly this way and that like ferrets stalking prey, working their way through the rain and mist, anxious to reach a myriad of destinations. They were eager for the warmth and dryness of home, to purge themselves of the cold and dampness chilling the inner recesses of their bodies.

To the right a stray dog huddled in a doorway across the street taking refuge from the elements. Its undernourished body quivered in the bone-chilling dampness. The canine's coat, a mottled grey, blended into the bleak surroundings. The mist digested the outline of the hapless figure – transforming it into a nonentity.

On the left a toddler and his mother, both dressed for the elements, made their way up the street. The little boy strained against his mother's grip as he stopped to splash in various pools of water forming on the sidewalk. A sense of déjà vu took over as Bud recalled his fondness for splashing in mud puddles and playing in the dirt when he was a wee tyke.

Next he expanded his gaze to incorporate the balance of the scene below. Fleeting images of cars and trucks appeared in the peripheral of his vision as they whistled along the slick street – on their way to any one of a multitude of locations. A muffled swish announced the arrival and immediate departure of each vehicle as it hissed its way into and out of his observational domain.

"Damn!" he uttered in a low growl, "Seattle is such a bloody wet and miserable place during the winter!"

A pattern formed on the window as shiny beads of moisture rapped against it, clung, momentarily suspended and dispersed into tiny rivulets cascading down the pane.

Suddenly he heard a deep, growling rumble coming from the darkened sky – his apartment shook in response. A sharp flash of blinding light quickly followed – the lightning emerged to play a role as co-star of the evening's theatrical performance.

Following this multi-sensory display the pounding rain continued incessantly, droning on and on, inducing in Bud a hypnotic trance. His mind was caught up in the action, focusing solely on the window – oblivious to all else. The elements conspired to sweep him away from his work through a continuous, pulsating beat against the glass. Immersed in the spell, Bud's thoughts drifted to more pleasant surroundings – the soothing warmth and sensuous sweetness of Hawaii.

****

Bud pictured himself languishing contentedly on his back, prostrate on the sands of Kuhio Beach – warm sun penetrating his body, the tang of salt air lingering in his nostrils, and the erotic view of bikini-clad beauties surrendering their bodies to the warmth of the sun.

What a vision, what a gorgeous vision!

Bud's upper lip quivered expectantly and a smile formed on his face as he settled into a state of utter bliss. His escape into paradise began to form as shapes emerged and transformed into vivid images in his mind. Through this sojourn his thoughts took flight, soaring temporarily from the sobering effects of reality.

Immersed totally in his dream, Bud could see, hear and smell the essence of Waikiki. Now he was sitting, oblivious to current surroundings, on his perch at Kuhio Beach.

To his left lay the majestic beauty of Diamond Head, visible to all subjects in its domain. Directly ahead he drank in the grandeur of the Pacific Ocean, a blend of bluish hues crowned by snow white caps on its waves. On the right he was rewarded with an unsurpassed view of the Pink Palace itself, the Royal Hawaiian, nestled among its common subjects – the other hotels on Waikiki Beach.

The sojourn into paradise served its purpose as it blanked out the dank grey scene and bone chilling dampness greeting him through the window. It was a welcome respite from the elements and other problems at hand; one he wanted to savor as long as possible.

Suddenly a door slammed shut! The spell was abruptly broken. The building shuddered and groaned in defiance.

****

"My God, it's freezing out there!" Tina bellowed. **"It's a son-of-a-bitch!"** She yanked off her boots and threw them helter skelter into the closet. "How's your work coming? I hope you're not taking any with you when we leave for Hawaii. Remember, you promised me!"

Tina's voice took on an accusatory tone as her eyes met Bud's glazed stare. It was obvious that he had been daydreaming again instead of working on his report for the office. She wanted him to get his ass in gear and complete the work before leaving.

"Don't worry, dear. This year I'm completing all my reports and projections before we leave." A hint of annoyance accompanied his voice, resulting from the harsh intrusion into his pleasant flight into fantasy. He had sought only a brief respite from reality to precede the real thing scheduled to take place in a few days. It annoyed him the way Tina had a habit of jumping in and shattering his daydreams.

Over the last five years trips to Hawaii had become an annual event for Bud and Tina. They provided a welcome sanctuary from the chilling rain and snow of Seattle's winter and were looked forward to expectantly well before the scheduled departure date. Each of the previous trips, however, had been compromised by the paperwork Bud inevitably took with him.

This year would be different! Bud had promised Tina. To hell with the office! No work would be brought!

"Bud, d'you realize we have only three more days before we're off to Hawaii?" Tina cried excitedly. "What're you looking forward to most?"

"Sun, booze and broads," he teased. His mind flashed back to Kuhio Beach and the tantalizing view of scantily clad female bodies.

He knew it would be touch and go whether he could complete enough work during the next three days to allow the luxury of no paperwork during the coming holiday. This possibility, however, wasn't shared with Tina. It would only upset her. Last year she had been irritated when he spent most mornings huddled over the kitchen table in their rented condo by the beach surrounded by paper. He didn't share her concern, however, since there had still been time for afternoons at the beach and visits to the local pub, the Melting Pot.

Ah, the Melting Pot! Its atmosphere dripped of adventure and intrigue. The Mai Tais were incredible. Although the origin of the bar's name was unknown to its current inhabitants, Bud surmised it was due to the diverse collection of colorful characters that frequented it over the years.

In Bud's mind the paperwork routine was not really that unpleasant ... it did, however, keep the office an active participant in their vacation. Although he didn't mind this imposition, Tina resented it deeply. Last year Bud had kidded her about the benefits she derived from his practice. He claimed tongue in cheek that she should be pleased since it didn't give him time to frequent the 'ladies of the night' who pedaled their wares on Kalakaua Avenue. In response Tina erupted into a tirade. She berated him, his "goddamned" office, and the "tight-assed broads" who frequented the street. Afterward she stormed over to the Melting Pot and drank with her friends from the beach. It wasn't until the wee hours of the morning that she returned to the condominium. As a peace offering Bud had promised to leave his work at home the following year.

* * * * * * * * * * *

Earlier Vacations

To put their upcoming vacation into perspective, Bud's thoughts flashed back to earlier years when annual vacations were limited to simple, inexpensive camping trips – in those days it was all they could afford. The trips were restricted geographically to a region in the Pacific Northwest. The area was bounded by Vancouver in Canada to the north, Portland to the south and Yakima to the east. The western side of the rectangle was the Pacific Ocean – a natural boundary. Within this perimeter they explored the wonders of the region – camping in the gigantic rainforests of the coastal northwest, squatting on farmers' pastures in the interior areas of Washington State and on occasion sleeping overnight in supermarket parking lots.

Bud treasured the outdoors. He loved tramping through lush evergreen forests, savoring the soothing fragrance of pine needles and the stillness that prevailed. In this environment only the occasional chirping of birds broke the intimate relationship between man and nature. It was a therapeutic experience, contrasting sharply with the hustle and bustle of the city. In this setting the sweet, musty aroma of moss enveloped the air and the delectable taste of wild salmon berries tempted his taste buds – adding to the multi-sensory collage.

It was exhilarating! He drank in the cool crisp air of the countryside with deep and greedy gulps, in contrast to inhaling the heavy and stifling atmosphere which enveloped the city. He woke to the joyful chirping of birds rather than to the tinny sound of an alarm clock. He examined the intricate changing patterns emerging from the glowing embers of a campfire, rather than the shallow, routine antics displayed on a television screen. In this setting, Bud was in his glory. He was born to live in close proximity to nature and looked forward to these annual visits to pay it homage.

In the beginning, Tina tolerated the annual trek into the wilderness. Although she knew Bud enjoyed it immensely, she could not generate the enthusiasm needed to fully share it with him. Tina hated the hard ground sheet which she slept on fitfully each night while dreaming of bugs, bears, and sundry wildlife which could threaten her existence. No wonder, she surmised, that Bud woke up early each morning tingling with excitement. However, in her opinion he rose early to escape the goddamn lumpy bed and the tingling was thanks to the cold, clammy dampness of the morning.

She hated, with a vengeance, the flies and bugs who always shared their vacations. While most campers rated campgrounds on the basis of proximity to lakes, showers, electricity and other amenities, Tina applied her own rating scale – based on bug density. Large quantities of mosquitoes rated a minus ten, black flies a minus five and so on. With this scale no campground could ever receive a positive rating from Tina.

BUD'S EARLY DAYS

* * * * * * * * * * *

Bud was not his real name. He was christened Robert, Alden Topper ... R.A.T. for short. Needless to say, the acronym did not please him and he vigorously discouraged its use as a nickname. Often, as a child, his displeasure was conveyed to peers though lightening-fast fists. As a small child he usually answered to adults as either Bobby or Robby – his favorite being Bobby. Bud's current nickname had evolved as a result of a nervous reaction he experienced when flustered or embarrassed. When he felt uncomfortable his face flushed and his voice stammered. This affliction was brought about when adults in authority spoke to him directly. When asked his name he would blurt out: **"B-b-b-b-b-b-b-b-b-d-d-d-d-y-y-y-y-y!"**

As a result of this pronunciation, Bobby evolved into Bud, a name he carried into his adult years.

Bud's enthusiasm for the outdoors grew out of childhood experiences. As a young boy he was raised in Grants Pass, Oregon, the son of a hunting guide and trapper. From the age of 10 he often joined his father on treks into the wilderness. Hunting and fishing became the love of his young life and he longed for school vacations which freed him to join his father on camping trips. He quickly gained expertise in setting camp, ferreting out edible foodstuffs from the surrounding woods, and tracking animals. Cubs and Boy Scouts were not for him ... he was where the real action was. Books, sports, and girls were distant seconds on his list of priorities.

Shortly after his thirteenth birthday Bud discovered girls. It was an awakening he never forgot. Prior to this event he had little time for them since they couldn't play football and weren't interested in tramping around in the forest. On occasion, however, he found himself daydreaming in school, staring with wonder at those bumps protruding from their sweaters – especially those belonging to Diane Grey. They were magnificent! So perfect, so firm and so huge. He fantasized about them. How they looked and felt. These thoughts were usually accompanied by a stirring in his loins, something he didn't quite understand. During these times his face turned crimson and he stammered when he spoke – his infliction intact. In these instances he was acutely embarrassed by thinking others knew what was on his mind.

It was on a warm day in July, during one of his frequent hikes into the hills, when the big event took place. Bud was playing the role of a big game hunter, stalking imaginary prey along a gently flowing creek. The pale blue water danced in the sunshine as the creek meandered slowly through the woods. Dark shadows and bright golden rays of sunshine intermingled among the huge fir trees in the dense forest, as they weaved intricate patterns of light and darkness. Bud knew what lay ahead as he worked his way along the bank of the stream.

A small waterfall was located just around the next bend; at its base was a deep, clear pool of water. Fish congregated there. Only last week he had caught several brook trout at the base of the fall. They were a good size, each measuring about eighteen inches in length. Their underbellies were a golden hue with a slightly red tinge blended in. The sleekness of their backs and tails were speckled with small black dots.

Fantastic! He licked his lips as the sight and smell of golden-brown, pan fried trout formed in his mind. The pink flesh melted in his mouth. Suddenly a different sound caught his attention. Bud froze – his ears instantly alert. It sounded again. This time the sounds of girlish laughter cut through the air. It was coming from the direction of the waterfall.

"Damn!" he cried aloud. "Girls've found my secret place."

He was annoyed. Although their bodies intrigued him, girls were a pain in the ass. They thought they were so grown up, whispering and giggling in groups of two or three. Most girls in his class talked about older boys all the time, viewing their male classmates as pests for whom they were far too worldly. Besides, Bud thought, their long dangling earrings, thick lipstick, and rouge looked ridiculous. God, they were a nuisance.

He thought of turning back, but curiosity won over. Who were they? What were they doing in his secret spot? The laughter and shouting increased in volume, overcoming the roar of the waterfall as Bud drew nearer.

Bud could hardly believe his luck, right before his bulging eyes frolicked three beautiful girls – stark naked. Except for imagining the female parts hinted at in underwear ads in the Sears catalogue, Bud had never actually seen a grown female body before. It was just like he had imagined – only better, much better. They couldn't see him as he was settled into his vantage point.

His heart beat so loudly he thought it could be heard over the roar of the waterfall and the sounds of the girls. Bud's breath came in quick gasps and a dry throat complemented his red face. A sensuous spell tightly gripped him, like a vice, as his eyes darted from one glistening body to another. He was mesmerized as his eyes focused on firm breasts that bounced saucily as they moved and the furry down covering their pubic areas. Eventually his eyes found their faces. Two he recognized as seniors at school—one starred on the basketball team—but he had never seen the third girl before. She had the largest tits he had ever imagined and he noticed that the blonde hair on her head didn't match the rest of her.

Suddenly the bulge thrusting out from the area of his groin demanded attention of its own. He had experienced this sensation before, but not what came next. His body shuddered as a strange force took him in its grasp, lifting him, soaring above the tree tops. Consciousness returned in an instant as the presence of a sticky wetness encompassed him. He lay there exhausted, not fully understanding what had happened. Interest in the girls suddenly waned and he made a quiet exit, leaving their modesty intact.

* * * * * * * * * * *

A Tragedy in Bud's Young Life

Tragedy struck shortly after Bud's fifteenth birthday. He and his father were riding in the family pickup truck along a narrow, winding back road high up in the mountains. They were returning from what had been an unsuccessful hunting trip, anxious to get home for a hot shower and mother's delicious cooking. The rain pelted down as large puddles formed in the gravel on the roadbed. At times the height of the water reached the axles, causing the driver to swerve abruptly, right or left, to avoid the deepest spots. A steep drop on the right hand side of the road governed the extent to which the truck could move in that direction.

Although it was still afternoon ominous black clouds darkened the sky, bringing on the darkness of evening. Suddenly a large buck deer lunged out of the dense underbrush, directly into the vehicle's path. On impulse Bud's father quickly swerved to the right in an attempt to avoid contact. The truck lurched off the road and barreled down a steep embankment. The jerking, bumping ride threw both of them about the cab like rag dolls. It flipped end-to-end several times before coming to an abrupt halt, at the base of a huge fir tree. Bud's father was killed instantly, his chest crushed by the engine that had been driven into the front seat. Bud, on the other hand, was fortunate. Instinctively he dove onto the floor when the truck careened over the embankment and avoided direct impact from the engine. He lay there, bleeding and semiconscious, for several hours before a forest ranger arrived at the gruesome scene.

A New Type of Life for Bud

With the death of his father Bud's young life was shattered. His frequent visits to the outdoors ended when, shortly afterward, he and his mother moved to the city of Portland. The rest of his youth was spent in the town with few opportunities for extended trips into the woods – still in relatively close proximity.

Bud's attention now focused on the football field. His speed, strength and size, coupled with quick reflexes made him a natural at either the halfback or fullback position. In Grade 10 he made the starting line-up for the senior team and quickly became the star – setting several school records by his senior year. He relished the attention and admiration resulting from his prowess on the football field – especially the adulation girls showered on him. He was obsessed with the cheerleaders and would visualize the girls at the waterfall as he watched them wiggle their butts during routines. With the confidence he had gained on the football field, Bud seldom stammered anymore. His face continued to glow red, however, whenever he spoke to beautiful members of the opposite sex.

In Bud's senior year the school team was in the running for the state championship. With only one league game left prior to appearing in the zone finals, the coach arranged for an exhibition game against an obscure school on the coast of Washington state.

"What do we need this for? Why play some hick team and risk injuries before the playoffs?" Bud asked the coach.

"Because you're too bloody cock-sure of yourselves," he replied. "We need this type of game to run some new plays and to give the second stringers more experience."

The team arrived in Hoquiam, Washington late on a Friday evening. The next morning they were scheduled to play Waglisla High School, a small relatively unknown school attended by Native Indians and whites in approximately equal proportions.

"This'll be a pushover!" Bud announced in the dressing room.

The other players gave the thumbs up sign in return. They also wanted to get the game over with and back to where real football was played.

During the warm-up Bud became infatuated with Waglisla's cheerleaders. One, in particular, stood out. She had great legs and boobs but it was something about her flippant manner that attracted him. She controlled all of the routines and set the tone for the rest of the girls. When she noticed him staring at her she stuck her nose in the air, flipped her ponytail and abruptly turned her back to him. He shrugged his shoulders, returning half-heartedly to the simulated practice routines.

As the game progressed, Bud's team received the shock of its life – these guys were no pushovers. The lead changed hands several times and by late in the fourth quarter Waglisla held the lead by four points. With only ten seconds remaining, the Oregon team gained control again and the quarterback handed the ball off to Bud. He faked to his left and spun a 90 degree turn to the right, leaving his check grasping at thin air. Now the real Bud sprang into action.

Now I'll show 'em! he thought as he galloped toward the goal line.

He sidestepped a second tackle, straight-armed another, and streaked along the sideline with only daylight between him and the goal posts. Suddenly he tripped, falling head over heels and short of the goal line.

The whistle blew. The game was over – HE LOST!

What the hell did he trip over? Bud looked around dejectedly until his gaze settled on the foot of one of Waglisla's cheerleaders, still strategically placed over the sideline and onto the field of play. The referee hadn't seen it, but now Bud knew what had stopped him.

The cheerleader walked over, a sympathetic look on her face and a twinkle in her eye. Her hand extended outward to offer him assistance to get up. It was the same one who had intrigued him earlier.

"Hi!" she announced with a curt flip of her head. "My name's Tina."

TINA'S EARLIER YEARS

* * * * * * * * * * *

Tina was a full-blooded American Indian raised in a small coastal community in Washington State. She was proud of her race and traditions, but wrestled with a love-hate relationship between supporting the Indian way of life on one hand and distancing herself from nature and the environment on the other. She vigorously defended traditions and the infrastructures which bonded Indian society, yet in recent years did not feel close to the outdoors. Hunting, fishing, and living off the land no longer appealed to her.

She had a mind of her own with aspirations to go far in the outside world. Her parents, brothers and sisters were all involved in various hunting and fishing activities – several were commercial fishermen and trappers. None of these pursuits, however, interested Tina. She wanted to observe, taste and experience all that life had to offer. There was so much to see and do, and so little time to do it.

As a small child Tina had been much closer to nature. She often romped through the woods, exploring the outdoors with other kids in the village. These activities provided her with an escape from school, an experience she didn't care for. Although never partial to animals she tolerated them at that time in her life, since many of her friends owned dogs and cats.

Tina's first experience at school in Grade 1 was memorable in that she spent the first month in the cloakroom – refusing to venture into the classroom where that white lady who hated Indians held court.

Eventually she was coaxed out of the cloakroom and into the area where the other kids played and learned.

On one occasion she vividly remembered her reception from the teacher after a class picture had been taken. Tina wasn't in the mood for picture taking and had a frown on her face at the moment the camera was snapped. After the picture was developed the teacher often referred to Tina as "the girl who doesn't smile." This salutation became the teacher's ongoing reference to her, often in front of her classmates.

On another occasion Tina raised her hand with one finger protruding (the signal that she would like permission to leave the room to pee). It was almost an hour before the teacher acknowledged her signal. By that time a puddle had formed under Tina's desk and she no longer needed to leave for the washroom. As a result Tina's opinion of her Grade 1 teacher was not complimentary. In the presence of friends and family Tina referred to her as, "The bitch."

The rest of her elementary school years were non eventful. Her teachers were okay and she attained slightly above average marks.

At the beginning of her secondary school years, Tina gained favor with the principal. He appreciated her independent nature and sense of responsibility. She was rewarded with baby sitting assignments for the administrator and his wife – this was a real coup! It came with prestige and real money. However, her babysitting assignments soon ended when she lost one of the principal's kids when they were walking in the woods.

The little bugger decided to play 'Find me if you can'. Tina didn't think it was such a big deal. *They found him later didn't they?* Nevertheless, this ended her babysitting career.

Soon afterward Tina developed an aversion to school – especially English class. She hated that subject with a passion. It was a monotonous bore demanding the writing of painful essays, meaningless recognition of parts of speech, and the mindless memorization of boring poems. Her written assignments were usually handed in late and were returned smothered in red ink. Each year after summer vacation, she dreaded the redundant annual assignment to write an essay explaining what she did during the holidays.

Why did English teachers always assign that topic? What a way to turn students off right at the beginning of the school year.

On the first day of school in her Grade 10 year she apprehensively entered English class to see who the teacher was. She didn't care who it was as long as it wasn't that old battleaxe, Miss Teeple. God, she hated that bitch!

When Tina arrived at the classroom door she couldn't believe her eyes. A vision of grandeur stood in front of the classroom. Instead of crotchety old Miss Teeple, the godlike figure of an Adonis surveyed the class. She rubbed her eyes in disbelief.

"Welcome to English class, miss," he addressed the mesmerized girl. "And what is your name?"

"T-t-t-tina!" she blurted out. A crimson warmth rose in her cheeks as he smiled in her direction. His ivory teeth, set evenly in a pair of sultry lips, glistened at her in regal splendor. She melted away. What a hunk!

"Pleased to meet you Tina. My name is Fred – Fred Formby. Do you enjoy English class?"

"L-l-l-love it!" she lied.

From that moment Tina's interest in English took an upward spiral – from the depths of Hades to the height of Mount Everest.

And that was not all. The tight pants Mr. Formby wore fascinated Tina. From the rear they silhouetted a firm set of buns and from the front they accentuated a strategic bulge. Tina gained a new interest in life. The hell with the woods! There was enough undiscovered terrain in English class to hold her interest from now on.

This was a new leaf in Tina's life which would lead her to unexpected experiences beyond her small coastal community. Her interest in other aspects of school also improved. Before long she became absorbed in a variety of activities including the future teachers' club and the cheerleading squad.

* * * * * * * * * * *

Back to the High School Football Game

It was shortly after tripping Bud on the football field that Tina and Bud became an item. He looked up at her as she smiled, saucily tossed her ponytail and waved her pom poms. At first he was very angry about the trip that cost him the football game. But then he was drawn to the languid brown eyes that gazed down at him. They mesmerized him – drawing his soul into their inner depths. Suddenly all motion ceased as they both stared into each others eyes.

"Hi, I'm Bud," he responded lamely.

They exchanged phone numbers and a long distance romance started. It began with a series of phone calls between Portland and Hoquiam. Then it blossomed into secret get togethers, half way between, in the city of Eugene. After high school graduations they enrolled in the same college and the liaison continued through to college graduation.

Soon after they were married and a life of adventure began together.

JANICE AND BEN ARRIVE ON THE SCENE

* * * * * * * * * *

The Toppers first met Janice and Ben White while on one of their annual camping trips at an unexpected stop at a campsite in north central Washington.

Bud had been anxious to make it to their next planned stop in the Canadian Okanagan valley as he pushed the camper to its limit on the winding highway. Angry storm clouds brewed overhead and a stillness in the dry air promised an abrupt change in the weather.

"It's getting dark, Bud, why don't we just stop at the next campsite?"

"'Cause I want to make it to the Canadian border."

"Why?"

"'Cause, that's why."

A flash of lightning accentuated the statement as if giving legitimacy to his position. Tina, however, didn't interpret it that way.

"See even God thinks you're a dummy. We've been on the road since early this morning and I'm tired. I want to pull over." Tina wasn't buying.

Suddenly a tremendous thunderclap endorsed Tina's position.

"Don't piss me off, Bud! I want to turn off."

"Awright! Awright!"

With a shrug of his shoulders Bud surrendered. There wasn't much point in arguing since it would only result in a vendetta of silence for the rest of the evening. He was well aware of Tina's temper when she didn't get her way.

"Look! Look!" Tina squealed excitedly. "There's a campsite up ahead."

Bud eased up on the gas pedal as the camper began to slow down on its approach to the turn off. They lurched to the right onto a bumpy dirt road leading off the highway just as the rain started. Soon a deluge poured from the sky – coming down in sheets, inundating the ground.

"It's just pelting down. Now aren't you glad I insisted we stop? At least we have a dry camper. Not like last year when you made me stay in that goddamn tent. Could you imagine us in that tent in this rain? I couldn't imagine it. Could you? This sure as hell isn't the Hilton, but it's better than a leaky tent. Don't you think so Bud?"

Bud just let Tina ramble on as he looked for a campsite in the torrential downpour. He wouldn't set up tonight – just find a spot, run like hell to the back of the unit, and jump into the dry interior.

Eventually he found a campsite to his liking and they pulled in.

"I'll go first to unlock the door," he ordered. "You follow after me so you won't get too wet."

By this time the rain had eased up and the Toppers both managed to make it into the camper without getting completely drenched. Bud had to admit to himself that the camper was sure a lot more comfortable than the tent used in previous years. However, he wasn't about to admit this to Tina.

They had settled in and were ready for a bite to eat when a commotion erupted from the adjoining campsite.

"You dummy, I thought you could light a fire! I thought you were an eagle scout when you were a kid," a woman's voice screamed through the underbrush. **"Besides this goddamn tent leaks."**

"Dry up. I'm doing my best!" a response shot back.

"I told you I didn't want to camp. This is the goddamn pits. I want to go to a motel. You know, you're a pain in the ass. I would rather spend this holiday in the bingo hall."

Tina's ears perked up at the last comment. Bingo was dear to her heart.

"See Bud, they sound just like us. Now that the rain has stopped we should go over and meet them." Tina quickly opened the door and shot through the underbrush into the next campsite... without regard for the dreaded flies or bugs ... Bud followed.

"Hi guys, my name's Tina! Don't worry about your fire I'll get my husband to light it for you."

"Oh, hi," came a sheepish response. Caught off guard, the couple suddenly realized their bickering had been overheard.

"My name's Janice and this is Ben."

It was the beginning of a new friendship; destined to grow out of similar likes and dislikes. Both women loved bingo and hated camping – conversely both men hated bingo and loved camping. A compromise was reached in which the women frequented bingo halls while the men stayed home or else worked. Camping became passé, replaced with stays at hotels or exotic vacation complexes. Annual vacations soon became trips to Hawaii.

Several of Tina and Bud's friends from Seattle made the annual pilgrimage to Hawaii at the same time of year. Their arrival at the beach was looked forward to by some of the Hawaiian locals whom they had befriended over the years. The Hawaiians nicknamed this enclave of visitors the 'Snowbirds'. The Islanders were used to seeing the 'white' mainlanders fly in during December and the same 'brown' ones fly out in January.

Janice and Ben White were among the members of this group. They always planned their visits to Hawaii to arrive first and depart last. Ben managed to arrange this schedule since he accumulated more holiday time than the others. This arrangement provided Ben with an opportunity to kid the others when it came time to leave the warmth and sun of Hawaii for the cold and wet of Seattle. He got his jollies by putting on a command performance at this time, waving goodbye to the others as they left on their return trips.

It drove Bud mad!

* * * * * * * * * * *

Ben was captain of a tugboat which plied the waters of Puget Sound, a waterway located in the northwest coastal region of Washington State. Occasionally he made extended hauls to Alaska. On these long runs he managed to accumulate additional holiday time. Janice often accompanied him on local trips but refused to go on the lengthy Alaskan run. When Ben went on these runs Janice and Tina made nightly tours of the bingo halls in the Seattle area.

PREPARING TO LEAVE
FOR HAWAII

* * * * * * * * * *

The time for Tina and Bud's next visit to Waikiki approached quickly. With only three days to go before holiday time, activity and excitement began to build. Tina feverishly sent out Christmas cards, bought gifts for relatives and friends, and planned for the holiday. The routine proved taxing since she also had a full time job to attend to and yet felt compelled to also fit in as many bingo games as possible before departure. Bud, on the other hand, worked hectically on reports and budget projections for the office and attended numerous Christmas functions. He lived in a state of constant apprehension as Tina wreaked havoc on their credit cards.

The night prior to departure finally arrived. Tina, who had been extremely busy earlier in the day, insisted on going to a restaurant for a final dinner before the next day's flight to Hawaii. Bud was agreeable since he did most of the cooking at home anyway.

When it came time to choose a restaurant, Tina insisted on a fancy one which catered to a select clientele. She chose an exclusive French bistro located at the north end of the city. This decision wasn't popular with Bud since it required formal attire and would be expensive. He hated to dress up for dinner since he wore a suit and tie to work every day and, when away from the office, liked to lounge in a grungy old pair of workpants. Tina referred to these pants as a 'decrepit rag' and had attempted to throw them out on several occasions. Each time, however, Bud managed to retrieve them from the garbage can before the city refuse collectors picked them up.

Bud and Tina were met at the restaurant by a dour faced maître d'. His haughty manner immediately annoyed Bud.

"Do Madame and Monsieur have a reservation?" came the stock question.

"Not me, but Tina does and it's a big one," Bud quipped, referring to the Indian Reservation from which she came.

This attempt at humor was lost on its intended recipient and a blank stare was returned in response. Without comment the maître d' picked up two menus and gestured toward an empty table.

It was a very elegant restaurant, decorated tastefully and likely at great expense. The other diners were dressed to the hilt; in contrast Bud wore an old, frayed sport coat – a favorite of his for the last twenty years. He had also managed to slip into his workpants before leaving the house while Tina was occupied with last minute preparations. A sweatshirt and pair of battered sneakers completed his outfit. Bud deliberately chose this attire to bug Tina for selecting such an expensive restaurant. It was likely his appearance which drew the hostile reception from the maitre d', supplemented then by disapproving glances from other diners near their table. Bud didn't care. He was making a point to Tina.

Examination of the menu and wine list confirmed his suspicions. Prices for the entrees alone were exorbitant and the wine list was out of sight. However,

Bud had anticipated this and, in his frugal way, was prepared for it.

After an exceptionally long wait a waiter finally arrived. This delay added to the tension of the moment. Finally they placed their order: two entrées and two empty wine glasses. Bud was ready. He had concealed a bottle of homemade wine in his bulging sport coat. The bottle, sporting a hand written label, attracted attention from some of the other diners seated nearby who turned up their noses before proceeding with their dinners. This slight was lost on Bud whose prime objective was to get out of the restaurant with as little financial damage as possible.

After delivery of the food the Toppers began to enjoy their dinner. Everything went smoothly until the ambience of the restaurant was shattered by a bloodcurdling scream, originating at the Topper's table.

"Shit, goddamn shit!" Tina screamed

Diners at the surrounding tables stopped with forks raised half way to their mouths!

"What's wrong, what's wrong?" shrieked the maitre d', appearing at the table instantly, his superior manner completely crushed.

"There's a hair in my food!" Tina roared. **"What kind of a joint're you runnin' here? Why does this always happen to me?"**

"We're not paying!" Bud hollered immediately seizing the moment. "Come on Tina, we'll go to MacDonald's to get a decent meal." He felt fortunate since this could be a money-saver for the upcoming holiday.

They were quickly ushered out of the restaurant amid much bowing, accompanied by hushed apologies. The staff was anxious to get the noisy couple out before other diners became upset. Bud smiled to himself, pleased that Tina's discovery hadn't taken place until after most of their meal was consumed. This saving would come in handy for their upcoming visits to the Melting Pot.

The big day finally arrived! At the sound of the alarm they were up with a start. The feverish race to get ready, complete the packing, and check out the house was underway. Doors were flung open and the contents of closets thrown into over-packed suitcases. Dresser drawers were emptied, and windows and doors bolted. After some delay they were finally ready. Fifteen minutes behind schedule they jumped into a cab, ordered the driver to put his foot down, and screeched down the street in the direction of the airport.

Hawaii, here come the Toppers!

CHAPTER 2

Arrival on the Scene

Late, as usual!
Bud was convinced the cab was programmed to hit every red light between home and the airport. It inched its way through the traffic, painfully crawling along one block at a time. He began to get panicky.

A hollowness etched itself deep in the pit of his stomach and beads of perspiration formed on his temple, their wetness leaving a cold sweat on his forehead. The dryness of Bud's mouth was accompanied by a thickness in his tongue, and when he swallowed his Adam's apple refused to work. Bud felt sick, just sick. He looked at his hand – it was shaking. Was he getting the flu? Maybe that wasn't so bad after all. Maybe his trip insurance would cover him for the loss and inconvenience. On second thought, probably not since he was still at his home base.

What if they missed the plane? Would they get a refund? Hell, he'd already paid the hotel in Waikiki, beginning tonight. Imagine – wasting all that money, first because Tina dawdled around so bloody much, and second because their cabbie drove like an old woman.

In Bud's mind he saw himself a spectator on the tarmac, watching helplessly as the plane took off. He could see the pilot in the cockpit, smiling and waving money at him through the window. That was Bud's money. Money he was losing because they were going to miss the goddamn plane.

"Can't you make this crate go any faster?" Bud demanded.

"An you'll pay my ticket, will ya buddy?"

"No way Mac! And my name's Bud, not Buddy."

"Who gives a shit?"

An ominous silence followed. Bud felt like wringing the cabbie's neck. No, better still get Tina to throw a few choice words his way. She had a real talent for that. But not until arrival at the airport, just in case they could still make it in time.

No way is this guy getting a tip, Bud thought aloud. The contemplation of at least some kind of saving helped a little to stem his growing disappointment. *Why are we in this mad rush?* he thought to himself. It happened time and again whenever they went on trips. It didn't matter whether they packed the day before or immediately prior to leaving the house, Tina always diddled around near departure time. In this case she had waited until the cab arrived at the door before deciding to floss her teeth. This habit of attending to last minute details during the crucial countdown period drove Bud mad. Why in hell did she make them late every time they went somewhere? Why did everything have to be done on her time?

Indian time, she called it.

Finally the taxi screeched to a halt in front of the entrance to the airport! Bud rushed out the door, slammed it shut, grabbed the luggage, waved off assistance from a skycap, and began running toward the check-in counter. He managed a series of neat moves while weaving through the crowd, luggage in hand. A tinge of nostalgia struck in spite of his sense of urgency. It was like old times, reminding him of the exhilarating sensation experienced on the football field in high school.

* * * * * * * * *

Bud was lost in thought as he snaked his way at top speed through the terminal. Now he was dribbling a basketball down the court at top speed, darting in and out among the opposing players. The old lady standing in front of the counter to the left, with the shopping bag in her hand, became his check. A deft move to the right with his head was followed by a dart to the left, and he quickly spurted around her.

Ha! he thought. *I faked her right out of her boots.*

The old lady glared after the fleeting figure as it disappeared into the crowd. **"Punk!"** she yelled after him. She should have stuck her foot out and tripped the idiot.

* * * * * * * * * * *

Reality suddenly hit Bud. He was in a crowded airport, laden with heavy suitcases, in danger of missing his plane, and 25 years older than he was acting. His shortness of breath quickly told the story. Tina was close on his heels, running through the terminal as if in the qualifying heat for the finals of a race.

Angry people were jostled as the couple continued scampering in and out of the mingling throng positioned between them and their destination. With chests heaving and sweat pouring off their faces they finally arrived at the ticket counter.

"Flight 509 to Hawaii!" he gasped breathlessly to the ticket agent. "We have three bags to check. You gotta get the lead out, man."

No response – the agent was busily talking to a colleague. It was something about a heavy date planned for next weekend and included graphic details on how he planned to seduce her.

"Hey wake up! Can't you see we're in a hurry?"

Again, no response – just a glance of annoyance focused in Bud's direction as the story continued.

"Goddamn it! Get your ass over here right now!"

This comment finally gained attention. The agent sauntered slowly over to the counter with a pained look on his face.

"You might just make it if you would only hurry, sir," he drawled sarcastically. "Smoking or non-smoking? Now, don't answer. Let me guess. Are you a smoker or not? Hmmmmmmm! Now let me see what we've got."

"We'll take anything. Just hurry with the boarding passes. We don't have time to piss around."

"I'm doing the best I can pal. You're the one who's late not me. Hey Stan, get a load of this one! He thinks it's our fault 'cause he's late. He's to blame and we're supposed to bust our ass."

"Don't get your shit in a knot, smart ass! Or I'll get my husband to report you," Tina jumped in.

"There you go lady. Departure gate 32. Have a nice day. My, my, what a pleasant couple."

"Up yours, you dink!"

They made it through the security check in record time. For once there was no line-up and Bud didn't set off the alarm from change in his pocket, his belt buckle or some other incidental item that caused the detector to beep. Thank God it didn't happen this time. They arrived a couple of minutes later, red faced and puffing heavily, at gate 32.

"Through here, hurry!" The attendant waved them in the right direction. "You'll just make it before the door closes."

The couple rushed down the aisle of the plane and, puffing hard and sweating profusely, plopped into their seats. They heaved sighs of relief as they buckled their seat belts. Just then the plane lurched forward and began moving toward the runway.

Whew! That was close! It's a good thing I packed last night. It's too bad you had to arrange for such a slow cabbie," Tina declared in an accusatory tone.

Bud didn't bother with a response. He just stared at the ceiling, twirling his thumbs and gritting his teeth.

The flight began in a routine fashion. After the customary instructions were given to buckle up and information provided on the locations of emergency exits the plane readied for takeoff. Clearance was given by the control tower and the passengers were thrust against the backs of their seats as the power of the engines propelled the plane down the runway and up into the atmosphere. It quickly gained altitude, leveled its flight path, and proceeded on its journey across the ocean.

Over the next two hours the cabin crew served breakfast, collected the trays and began a bar service. Things were going smoothly until half-way into the flight. At that point Tina noticed Bud ogling a well-endowed stewardess. The flight attendant innocently brushed her hip against his shoulder each time she passed down the narrow isle – **that type of hip check Bud didn't mind**. Out of the corner of his eye he watched her ass wiggle to and fro as she performed her duties.

"God, what an ass! The superstructure is great too," he muttered aloud to himself, leering down the aisle.

"Hey stewardess, another Mai Tai please!" he ordered.

This was heaven, pure heaven.

****

Bud was lost in thought, in a languid and mellow mood. Suddenly he found himself on a secluded beach with the stewardess, romping in the nude, chattering and giggling. Her breasts bounced in the breeze as they darted toward the ocean surf. The trace of a smile formed on his face as he imagined the fullness of her ripe, enticing body. He was half awake and half asleep, experiencing another world – then it happened. At first the sensation blended into the fantasy but it wasn't long before the sticky wetness on his legs grabbed his attention. Bud's dreamlike world came to a cruel and abrupt end.

Tina had poured her drink all over his lap.

"Sorry dear, the superstructure tipped," Tina hissed, her dark eyes blazing and a sarcastic smile on her lips.

"Bullshit! You did that on purpose just as I was calculating some figures in my head for a project at the office."

"It wasn't those figures that were in your head and wipe that stupid smile off your face!"

Two hours had passed since the incident and Bud's pants had dried and no longer stuck to his legs when he moved. The icky sensation had run its course and things were looking up as they both prepared subconsciously for their arrival in the tropical paradise awaiting them.

****

Thinking of Friends on Waikiki Beach

Tina's thoughts drifted off to her friends in Hawaii. Among them Terri the beach philosopher; and Pam and Alice, the two old ladies who spent every day at the beach looking for men on one hand and complaining bitterly about them on the other.

Terri spent every morning at the beach always attempting to get into everyone else's business. She offered her services as mother confessor to any of the beach people who wanted advice. Business from those who knew her, however, was slow. A religious zealot, she disapproved of many of the people and their antics. She had little time for the two old ladies whom, in her opinion, were cut from "rougher cloth" than she cared for.

Pam was the elder of the two old ladies. In her younger days, she had been an exotic dancer. Back then acts like hers only stripped down to a g-string, whereas nowadays the strippers took it all off. Girls currently in the business had no shame she thought. In her opinion, the business had seriously gone downhill since she was a star.

In contrast, Alice, the second old lady, had at one time almost been a nun. She gave up the calling, however, shortly after her pregnancy began to show. In contrast to her partner she was reluctant to compare current day clergy with their earlier counterparts.

Tina looked forward to spending time with all of them, gossiping alternately with Terri and the two old ladies. Since they sat in different locations on the beach it required constant shuffling from one spot to the other. In no time she would know all that had occurred in Waikiki since her last visit, what was currently happening there, and what would likely happen during the coming year. In return the other three women would know everything that had taken place in Seattle, what was taking place at the current time, and what would likely take place in the coming year.

****

In the meantime Bud's mind was busy planning his tan and scheduling walks with Ben, as part of their daily routine. He also thought of the Melting Pot and its assortment of characters – those constituents so integral to its decor. He wondered what force drew those colorful misfits, like a magnet, to the bar.

"I should write a book about that joint," he said to himself aloud. Deep down, however, he knew he would never get around to it.

"There it is! There it is!" Tina shouted excitedly. **"It's fantastic! Look at it, look at it!"**

The image of Diamond Head appeared at that moment in the window to the left of Tina's head. Its majestic features were complemented by the lush green hues provided by the vegetation which completely enveloped it. Adding to the magnificent view was the innate blue of the sky, contrasting sharply with the fluffy white clouds lazily drifting amidst it. The scene was breathtaking in its beauty, enhanced even more so by the harshly divergent images of Seattle's winter that still clung to the peripheral of their minds – the dull grays and greens of that city were far away from the magic of this wonderland.

By this time all passengers with window seats peered anxiously at the sight, sharing in Tina's enthusiasm. The majority of travelers, however, were in center or aisle seats, well away from the window. They looked left and right, some standing with craned necks, seeing little or nothing and smiling peevishly.

The plane took a wide sweep over the city of Honolulu and made its approach to the west of the airport. From the window Tina could make out the wide expanse of the cane fields in the countryside, the concrete ribbons of the city's freeways, and the memorial at Pearl Harbor. A smooth landing followed after which the plane taxied to its point of disembarkation. "Please remain in your seats until we have come to a complete stop!" came the announcement over the PA system.

Several passengers ignored the instruction as they rummaged in the overhead bins above. By the time the plane came to a complete halt almost everyone was in possession of their carry-on luggage and poised to lunge forward at the moment the outside door opened.

As the passengers and crew waited expectantly the walkway was readied for deplaning. Tina and Bud had maneuvered their way to the front of the line-up – ready to spring when the moment arrived.

As the door swung open a dazzling brilliance cascaded into the plane's darkened cavity. Eyes squinted in an attempt to become accustomed to the sudden brightness. A swarm of commuters quickly darted from the plane, enveloped by the sweet fragrance of Hawaii as they hurried along the walkway.

Tina and Bud's game plan called for a swift arrival at the carousel, a quick snatch of their luggage, a hasty retreat from the airport, and then a hurried rush to the beach – their ultimate destination.

Janice and Ben, who had arrived in Hawaii three days earlier, had promised to meet them at the airport. However, the Toppers weren't counting on that since they knew it depended upon two factors. One, that Ben wasn't nursing a hangover and the other, that he could borrow a car from one of the local characters at the Melting Pot.

The airport was jammed!

A sea of people milled around in the terminal, their dull drone overpowering any audible noise from the PA system. People filled every crevasse of the building making Bud feel claustrophobic. He felt hemmed in, unable to move freely. His arms hugged his sides as he stealthily foraged forward toward the luggage carousel.

It took all of Tina's skill, developed at year-end sales in Northgate Shopping Center, to maneuver her way through the throng of people. Bud arrived almost as quickly by charting a course through the tail stream left in her wake. After their successful arrival they awaited the luggage.

Finally, after what seemed like an eternity, the conveyer belt spit off the Topper's luggage. The bags began their circular route on the carousel beginning on the side opposite where they stood. Bud recognized their luggage immediately by the distinctive red patches Tina had sewn onto each of the handles to set them apart from others. She had done this to avoid a repeat of last year's experience when they took the wrong piece from the carousel. That mistake wasn't discovered until after their arrival at the condominium. As soon as he opened the suitcase Bud knew it wasn't theirs. But it took three days of inconvenience before an exchange was completed with the owner.

There's our luggage," Bud shouted over the din. "I wonder if the Whites are here to pick us up?"

"I don't see them," Tina replied as she surveyed the crowd.

Suddenly a piercing whistle shrieked through the terminal.

"Wheeeet! Wheeet!! Wheeet!!!"

The sound cut like a knife right through the crowd's clamor. All noise ceased as everyone looked for the source of the racket.

"Wheeeet! Wheeet! Wheeet!"

There it was again! The sound was piercing and some of the throng held hands to their ears to relieve the assault on their ear drums.

"What is it? What is it?" the old lady next to Tina screamed, holding onto her ears.

"Oh, it's just Janice!" Tina announced with a shrug.

WHEN JANICE AND BEN
FIRST MET

* * * * * * * * *

J anice came from a family with a background of female whistlers. Her maternal grandmother and mother were each capable of emitting a whistle so loud and piercing it could be heard for blocks. Janice, of course, did not take a back seat to any of her relatives in this department. She used her whistle for a variety of purposes: to direct traffic for events at her children's school, to make her presence known in a noisy crowd and to drown out Ben when she was pissed off with him for ignoring her and talking too much about ships to other mariners. On occasion she used this talent when the bingo halls, which she and Tina frequented, became too noisy to hear the numbers as they were called.

As a small child Janice loved music. Whenever a song was played on the radio she would dance to its beat. Swinging and swaying back and forth to slow tunes and jiggling up and down to the faster ones. Her parents got a kick out of how she would leap up from whatever she was doing to become totally immersed in the ritual. She often performed for company when they came to visit. Friends thought it was so entertaining that a small tyke would put such energy into her dance routines. Once she learned to talk Janice decided to add words to her act. She memorized the words to many songs and sang while she danced. At first everyone thought this was cute. However, it wasn't long before her audience dwindled since she sang so badly out of tune. By the time she was ready for kindergarten she had stopped the singing part of her act.

Throughout her elementary school years Janice continued to love music and, in secret, continued to dance. By this time her repertoire had expanded to include the jive and the twist. She knew her limitations, however, when it came to singing.

Whenever Betty, Janice's mother, heard a song she liked on the radio, she accompanied it with a low whistle which closely followed the melody. At first this habit annoyed Janice – she thought it spoiled the song and she wished her mother would stop. However, Betty was quite good at it. In fact her rendition of those songs which were whistling classics such as *Stardust* and *Smoke Gets in Your Eyes* were very well done. Betty could also emit a loud and sharp whistle when she wanted. This was frequently used to summon her husband or Janice when they were at a distance.

One day Janice surprised her mother by asking to be taught how to whistle. Later it was this skill that was instrumental in meeting Ben.

* * * * *

In those days Ben was a greenhorn crewman on one of the small tugs which worked the port of Seattle. The role of the boat was to jockey various floating objects around the harbor. Its tasks included assisting freighters in docking, nudging barges into their berths, and moving log booms from one location to another. His job included hooking tow ropes onto the winch and keeping them clear of the propeller, avoiding wrap arounds, and cooking for the skipper – the other half of the two man crew.

"Coil that goddamn rope in the other direction!" the skipper screamed at Ben. **"Bloody kids, they don't know anything anymore,"** he muttered as an after thought.

Ben quickly threw the rope in the tail stream of the tug to work out any kinks and began pulling it back in, coiling in the direction opposite to his earlier attempt. He wanted to do a good job since he liked the sea and the job paid well.

"Goddamn skipper!" he mumbled to himself, "he could be more subtle."

Ben recalled his first day on the boat, less than a week ago, when he was ordered to make lunch. He had rummaged around in the grub box and came up with two cans of soup. Good, he thought. He could make soup and sandwiches. Soon everything was going well with sandwiches made and the soup bubbling on the stove. It was important, Ben thought, to make a good first impression. He wasn't much of a cook but he had produced a masterpiece for the skipper. He even smothered the ham sandwiches with pickles and ketchup – his favorites.

Ben went to the wheelhouse and took over the helm as the skipper jumped back into the small galley. The deck hand smiled to himself as he steered the boat. This was his first day and things were going really well.

"Jesus Christ, what the hell is this?" boomed the raspy voice of the skipper from the direction of the galley. The sound of a splash followed as the pot of soup and tin cans were chucked into the water.

"What's wrong?" Ben asked meekly in a suddenly squeaky voice. Maybe the skipper didn't like pickles or ketchup.

"Listen kid, y' never, ever, open a tin upside down on a sea goin' vessel," the skipper roared back.

It was Ben's introduction to one of the cardinal rules of the sea. Except for the skipper's abrupt criticism from time to time things seemed to work out relatively well for the rest of the week. Actually, Ben surmised, his bark was worse than his bite. In fact he started to like the gruff old geezer.

Ben had been into the job a couple of months when the captain decided to tie up at a dock located at the foot of an abandoned warehouse. By this time the skipper had grudgingly acknowledged that young Ben had potential as a seaman and as a result a good rapport had developed between them.

"Wrap the line around the cleat at the end of the dock," the skipper ordered.

The deckhand dutifully nodded and jumped onto the dock from the bow of the boat with the tie-up rope in hand. A strong current was running which made it important to secure the boat at the bow first, so that a reversal of the engine would swing the rest of the vessel against the dock. The stern could then be secured as the next step. Just as he jumped onto the dock an ear piercing whistle shattered his ear drums.

"Wheeeet! Wheeet!! Wheeet!!!"

With his hearing impaired Ben lost his sense of balance. He tumbled head over heels into the murky water.

"What the hell's that noise?" the skipper bellowed. **"And Ben, what the hell're you in swimmin' for? We got work t'do – get out of the water this minute."**

A bewildered and drenched Ben crawled back onto the dock. He looked like a drowned cat – his hair matted to his face and water squishing from his boots. What the hell happened? What was that awful ear piercing whistle? He glanced up and could make out a figure standing on the warehouse loading platform above. It was a female and she was doubled over in laughter. As Ben continued to stare she composed herself and stood with her hands on her hips.

"Hi!" she shouted downward. **"How's the water? My name's Janice, what's yours?"**

****

Back to the Arrival at the Airport

"Over here! Over here! Hey, you guys, I'm over here!" Janice called excitedly, her arms flailing wildly.

People close to her scurried out of elbow range to avoid being hit by her piston-like movements.

"I hear her but I can't see her," Bud reported to Tina. "She's too short to be seen in this crowd and I don't see Ben anywhere."

"There she is!" Tina responded. Janice's hands and wrists were barely visible over top of the crowd scurrying to get out of her way. Tina hurried toward her leaving Bud to carry all of the suitcases and the two shopping bags by himself.

"Hi Janice, where's Ben?" asked Tina.

"Oh he's illegally parked, as usual. He went to put his fake press sign on the dash. Boy are you guys ever white! Look at how brown I am! I'm sure a lot browner than you. Look." She held out one of her lethal wrists for inspection.

By this time Ben appeared, wearing a hat similar to those used by Skycap luggage attendants. It was a hat he wore on the tugboat and he found it also came in handy for bypassing line-ups at airports.

"Hello, y'all!" greeted Ben. "Let's get the hell out of here before I get towed away. I'm in a Police only zone and my press sign may not work."

Ben and Bud carried the luggage to the car while the women chatted about news from Seattle and Waikiki. Although it had only been three days since the Whites and Toppers had parted company it could have been years, based on the extensive discussion in which the two women were deeply engrossed.

"My God, is this rust bucket safe?" Bud demanded. "I'm surprised it runs."

"I got a deal so quit complaining."

Next, Bud untied the rope used to keep the trunk shut. Gazing into the interior he could see it was filled to the top with old tires, batteries and empty beer bottles.

"There's no room in here for even one suitcase, let alone three, and two shopping bags," Bud blurted. "I guess we'll have to stack them in the car with us."

Janice and Tina entered the car first and then the men stacked the luggage around them. Since the driver's seat had to remain clear to enable Ben to drive most of the luggage ended up in the backseat with Tina. By the time it was Bud's turn to climb into the back there was almost no room left. It was a very tight squeeze but everyone managed to get on board.

Bud rode into Waikiki bent like a pretzel, his head touching his knees, his left leg falling asleep and his back in supreme agony. Suitcases and bags surrounded him, jabbing him in his legs, arms, neck, and back. In the meantime Ben enjoyed the ride into town as he told everyone of the great deal he got on the car through Rocco, one of the characters from the bar. Hell, he got the car for less than half the amount charged by legitimate rental companies.

Nothing in the car worked except the engine. The radio was broken, the windows wouldn't close, and the trunk and hood were both tied down with rope. Added to that, the car had a view of the roadway underneath them thanks to the holes in the floor boards.

At last they pulled up to the hotel complex. Bud's painful ordeal was finally over.

"Yeah Ben, you got one hell of a deal!" he cried sarcastically. As the door popped open he rolled painfully out of the backseat and hit the ground bent almost in half. Playing his condition for all it was worth Bud walked around the car and into the hotel lobby hunched over with his arms dangling on the ground. To gain attention he began beating his chest, mimicking an ape.

"It's those crazy snowbirds again," muttered one of the locals as Bud played his newly acquired disability to the hilt.

The Whites helped Tina and Bud move the luggage into their rented condominium on the 32nd floor of the building. Since the Toppers had made private rental arrangements with the owner they were not registered at the desk.

After several drinks to toast their arrival plans to go to the beach that day were abandoned. It was decided, instead, that Ben and Bud should go out to purchase groceries while the ladies continued their joint newscast.

Two hours later the men arrived back at the building laden with bags of groceries. "What room am I in?" Bud asked.

"How the hell should I know? Don't you know?" Ben responded.

"I can't remember which floor we're on let alone the room number. I didn't bring a key and we aren't registered at the desk."

Between them they could only recall the last two digits of the room number but not the floor. All they were sure of was that it was located somewhere between the tenth and thirty-eighth floors. So, beginning on the tenth floor the two men stopped the elevator at each successive level. One stayed in the elevator with the load of groceries while the other knocked on the door of the suite with the same last two digits of the room number.

An hour later they arrived, exhausted, on the thirty-second floor. Tina answered the knock.

"Where the hell've you guys been?"

"Never mind, it's bloody lucky there's an elevator. We need a drink."

CHAPTER 3

The Beach At Last

The sun slowly crept over Diamond Head as Bud stirred his way out of a fitful sleep. It had been a long night during which the clamor of traffic from the street below kept him constant company. He twisted and turned throughout the evening, holding a pillow over his head in a futile attempt to shut out the din. It didn't work. Honking horns and squealing tires intermingled with other noises of the night. Outside the bars the sounds of chattering and laughing contrasted with shouting and cursing, providing a dichotomous cacophony of noise.

He lay in bed for hours consciously absorbing every new sound wafting its way up to the thirty-second floor. A glance at Tina, fast asleep beside him, demonstrated complete disregard for the disruptions around her. He was envious of her deep and even breathing, a requisite to a restful and deep slumber.

"God!" he muttered to himself. "I came for a rest – to get away from the noise and bustle of Seattle. Now look't this bloody circus. It's the sounds of Waikiki alright, reverberating through a concrete jungle."

Finally he tossed the sheets aside and eased his way out of bed. His lack of sleep added further to the discomfort caused, in part, by remnants of a hangover thanks to all the Mai Tais he drank the night before. It must've been two or three o'clock in the morning before the Whites had finally left and wound their way over to the hotel they preferred to stay in each year.

He thought they'd never leave. Imagine staying up till all hours and drinking like a fish. Nothing like starting off the first day of your holiday feeling like a wet dish rag.

"Are you joining Ben this morning for your usual walk?" Tina's muffled voice was barely audible from under a tangle of bed covers.

"Not this morning. I want to ease my way into this routine one step at a time. I can't take it yet, I feel the pits." He gulped down two Anacins, hoping to ease the throbbing in his head.

Last night's drinking hung thick on his tongue as he pried open the door of the refrigerator and poured a glass of unsweetened grapefruit juice. His face instantly screwed up and his body quivered as he forced it down. Bud's dormant taste buds awoke abruptly from the sharpness of the fluid.

His next objective was to get the coffee pot ready without spilling grounds all over the counter. For some reason this task always proved difficult. Every time he scooped coffee out of the tin container to put into the filter, the counter became littered with coffee grounds. He swore the plastic scoops which came with tins of coffee leaked since it was never a clean operation.

After opening the cupboard above the sink Bud's hand groped for the familiar feel of a rectangular package of coffee filters. All thumbs, he managed to secure it in his hand and bring it down to the counter. Gingerly he placed a filter in the top of the coffee pot and quickly scooped in five heaped tablespoonfuls of coffee. As usual some grounds spilled on the counter and floor. Next he added the water needed to complete the task and turned on the switch. Soon the heavenly aroma of fresh coffee wafted its way into the room. Bud inhaled deeply as the bouquet permeated his nostrils and worked down into his chest. He smiled to himself as the fragrance added to the morning's ambience.

After filling his cup with coffee he eased over to the sliding glass door and stepped onto the lanai. A warm breeze greeted him. It was refreshing and just what he needed to regain some semblance of normality. The blue, red and green colors of the landscape were so vivid it was startling. At first their psychedelic impact assaulted his senses but he soon adjusted to it and came to marvel at the intensity of the beauty around him.

In the distance, the ocean, alive with motion, spit out white-capped waves on their shore bound journey. Sailboats dotted the skyline, white sails carrying them gracefully through the surf. Further along the panoramic skyline he could see the parachute of a para surfer billowing in the breeze with its human cargo dangling above the water like prey carried by a hawk in flight. Straining his eyes Bud could also see the dots of surfers bobbing in the ocean's wake, patiently waiting to catch the next big wave to glide in on a brief but exhilarating high.

Turning to his left he saw the bold outline of Hawaii's most famous landmark.

Diamond Head. It was superb!

Bud peered at the brashness of its silhouette defiantly jutting skyward into the grey mist of the morning. Peeking over its shoulder were orange and golden rays of shimmering light announcing the arrival of the sun. The pleasant coolness of the morning, combined with the awakening brilliance of colors, lost Bud in a spell of magic and beauty. His hangover temporarily forgotten, he drank fully of the vision's grandeur.

"Eeeyii! Eeeyii! A shrill scream suddenly shattered the stillness of the morning. **"Bud come here! Come here!"** Tina shrieked.

"What is it? What is it?" Bud blurted out in an alarmed voice as he dashed into the kitchen.

"Over there! Look over there! It's a bug, a goddamn bug!"

A small cockroach huddled in the corner of the kitchen sink – likely scared to death from the commotion.

"What'd you expect? You're in the topics aren't you?"

"I don't care; I want to move out of here! I don't do bugs!"

After a few minutes Tina calmed down realizing that the odd cockroach was the norm in this part of the world. As long as the unit was fumigated on a regular basis the bug problem was minimal. With this in mind Tina turned her attention to plans for the day.

"Vic and Ann want us to toast the sunrise with them before we head to the beach! We should be on our way as soon as we have breakfast. I want to get to the beach early. Did you make coffee? Come on Bud we need to get ready."

Tina was always in a rush when she looked forward to something, otherwise her movements were slow as hell. It was obvious that she wanted to arrive at the beach early in order to meet Terri, Pam, and Alice whom she hadn't seen since last year. A storm of gossip would ensue. Terri held court in her section of the beach while the two old ladies would simultaneously roam the outer perimeter of their own sector of waterfront. They found this patrol duty to be essential in order to intimidate unwelcome sunbathers who might encroach upon their part of the beach.

"I'll pick up my beach gear on the way to the seashore and meet you there around 10:00 A.M.," Tina announced to Janice with a click of the telephone. She then turned to her husband. "Bud, Janice says there's a special on my beach stuff at the ABC store. We should stop in on the way to the beach."

It was only a short walk from the condo to the beach front. Tina was in a hurry this morning but Bud knew that as the holiday progressed, she would cover the distance at an increasingly slower pace. By that time it became a painfully slow journey for anyone accompanying her. This morning, however, was different. Tina was flying as she crossed the street against the traffic light and barreled her way into the ABC store to pick up her beach things. She roared up to the cash register with her purchase under her arm and demanded that Bud pay the bill immediately.

He was then to get his ass in gear and carry it to the beach at top speed. She was worried that Janice may have already arrived to pick up on the scuttlebutt before her.

As usual Janice wasn't at the beach when the couple arrived. She and Ben were seldom on time, usually arriving one or two hours later than agreed upon. Their normal excuse was either an outing for breakfast which took longer than planned or Ben's chance meeting with someone who worked on the tugs back home – but Bud knew better. In spite of the close relationship between the two couples Ben frequently was involved in mysterious business deals. Once it was a new concept for an apartment complex, another time a secret marina. These morning business meetings usually involved Rocco.

* * * * * * * * * *

Ben's Involvement with Rocco

Whenever he was in Hawaii Ben spent a great deal of time with Rocco, one of the characters from the Melting Pot. It was rumored that Rocco had connections with the Mafia on the mainland and was involved in a number of clandestine activities on the island. On several occasions Bud warned Ben against developing a close relationship with this character but his advice fell on deaf ears. Ben found Rocco colorful and interesting; someone exciting who he wanted to maintain contact with.

Ben had always been a sucker for intrigue. As a youngster he listened with awe to stories of rum running days in the Puget Sound area during the prohibition era. His grandfather and other cronies used to spin yarns about ships during the 1920s, loaded with booze, running in the darkness of night without lights. They would pick up their cargo on the Canadian side of the border and thread their way through the San Juan Islands, watchful for the American coast guard. Men who played this dangerous game enjoyed an image far more adventurous and romantic than just one of common smugglers. The acceptance of rum running was partly due to the unpopularity of prohibition with many Americans of the day. A number of the famous and wealthy families of the Pacific Northwest originally got their start through involvement with the rum running trade.

* * * * * * * * *

Tina's Arrival at the Beach

Armed with her newly acquired gear, Tina wound her way through the prostrate bodies strewn over the beach, working toward the section guarded by Pam and Alice. She waved quickly to Terri – she would see her later. A short distance from her sat Mia, one of the bar's regulars who was catching some sun before reporting for duty on one of the bar stools. Tina would catch up with her later also.

Time was crucial; Tina had to catch up on all the news as quickly as possible. That meant frequent, intense visits with all of her beach buddies ... if only they got along among themselves. It was damn annoying to have to move regularly from one camp to another.

Appreciation of the sights on the beach definitely rest in the eyes of the beholder. On one hand Bud thought the blond lying near the edge of the water, wearing a bikini with a hint of delicate pink nipple showing through the sheer fabric on her top, added a touch of class to the scenery. Tina, on the other hand, thought the sight was disgusting. Instead, Tina's eyes focused on a well-muscled stud wearing a skimpy loin cloth—at best a tight fitting jockstrap—strolling along the edge of the shoreline. She thought the strategic bulge in his groin area was interesting; its humungous size evoked some curiosity in her mind. Bud was not impressed.

"What d'you think of that hunk?" Tina asked the two old ladies upon her arrival at their spot.

"He prob'ly couldn't handle us," Pam responded, a nostalgic tone to her voice. "They just don't make 'em like they used to."

"Christ," Bud cut in, "he could probably pole vault over the three of you with that dong. Besides he prob'ly likes boys."

At this point the figures of Janice and Ben appeared on top of the seawall. Janice began waving one arm, followed with a moderate whistle to announce their arrival; no point upsetting the beach by using full volume – that could wait for a more appropriate occasion.

Ben took up his usual residence on the bench next to the seawall. He spent most of his time on the bench which was shaded at this time of the morning. His skin was fairer than the others and could stand less exposure to the sun. Besides, there were other benefits which accrued to him from that vantage point. In that location he had an excellent view of all inhabitants of the beach and could quickly scan the area for women with the most intriguing bodies. Once they were identified he plotted the coordinates of their locations, as if at sea, and kept close track of their movement. The blond which had caught Bud's attention earlier was quickly picked up by Ben's skilful eye and her position accurately recorded on his chart.

Janice began making her way toward the old ladies' turf with beach gear under her arm. As she wound her way through the maze of sunbathers her excitement built at the prospect of once again sharing command of those sections of beach forming the camps of the other women. She also looked forward to gossiping for hours with the incessant discussion interrupted only by occasional dips to cool off in the pool.

Just before Janice arrived at the spot where Tina and the two old women were located, the stud in the jockstrap reappeared on his return walk. His head was held high and cocked to one side as he swaggered along the waterfront; conscious of the admiring stares from many of the women and the panting looks from that different group of men whose preference was boys. He was completely engrossed in himself as he provocatively shared glimpses of his perfect body with new-found fans along the beach. Lost in intimate thoughts of how he was God's gift to the opposite sex, the stud was oblivious to any other living soul, until Janice announced her presence to the entire beach.

"Wheet!!! ... Wheet!!! ... Wheet!!!" the shrill blast pierced the air like a knife. **"Hey, baby! You ... Yes,**

you ... the one with the balls hanging out! How would you like a bite of my bannock?"

Janice's broadcast gained the attention of everyone within ear shot as she addressed the hunk. Startled by this unexpected ambush, his swagger quickly disintegrated and a crimson tide surged across his face. He raced down the beach in embarrassment. The old women screamed with laughter as Janice arrived at their camp.

* * * * * * * *

Past Lives of the Two Old Ladies

The two old ladies were colorful characters with interesting pasts. Although she wouldn't admit it, Pam had been a professional stripper in her younger days. Following her work in this profession she spent several years as a masseuse in a body-rub parlor. She had invested her money wisely and was now spending her retirement years in Waikiki.

Alice, on the other hand, had worked at a number of occupations over the years. Immediately after completion of high school she began preparation to become a nun. However she left before completion of her vows, pregnant with a child. Afterward she held a number of jobs, including waitress, cab driver, and prison guard. She still worked part time as a cashier at the Food Basket supermarket on Kuhio Avenue.

It had been twenty years since Pam last exposed her buns professionally. When she worked as a stripper her stage name was Bunny. Few people outside her immediate family knew of her past profession since she often spoke of a late husband in an attempt to give others the impression that her previous occupation was that of housewife. In the beginning she attempted to maintain this facade with Tina and Janice, but one day during the previous year's visit, Alice confided to them that Pam had never married and was once a red-hot stripper. In her younger days she was billed as the next Gypsy Rose Lee. Although her body had thickened over the years there remained the hint of a once sensuous body. Her face, however, had toughened with time. Deep creases lined her features giving an intense and sinister appearance when she glared at anyone who displeased her.

Alice, on the other hand, had led a sheltered life during her younger years. Her schooling had been received at a convent and upon graduation from high school she decided to take up the calling. However, there was a rebellious streak in her which didn't lend itself to the principled life of a nun. She was often summoned by the headmistress to be disciplined because she was unable to maintain a Spartan lifestyle. Alice liked to regularly take more than just one nip of brandy at a time and had frequently experienced a stirring in her loins when she observed male bodies engaged in physical work or sports.

While still in high school she'd spent many hours watching the boys' basketball team from a nearby school practice for league games. One afternoon, after the practice was over, she walked by the boys' change room on her way out of the gym. The door was slightly ajar and out of the corner of her eye she could see some of the players stripping down to enter the shower. Her breath quickened and she tingled with excitement as naked figures, displaying their manliness, came into view – it was only a quick glance since she didn't dare linger, but it remained in her mind to tantalize and entice her. Before her vows were completed she became pregnant and that drastically changed her lifestyle.

* * * * * * * * * * *

Pam and Alice discouraged most trespassers on the beach by systematically patrolling the perimeter of sand they claimed as their own. Occasionally when non-observant sunbathers took up residence in that area the icy stares of the women were usually sufficient to dislodge them. On one occasion last year, however, the women had to rely on other tactics to preserve their territory.

In this instance they were infiltrated by a group of tourists who arrived and plunked themselves down on the women's sacred section of beach. You could tell they were recent arrivals from the mainland by their creamy white skin. Blankets, radios, cameras and picnic baskets were flung unceremoniously across the sand. The sounds of a blaring radio and the clink of liquor glasses, raised in unison to loud toasts, shattered the serenity of the women's domain.

Pam and Alice immediately employed their usual defensive tactic by staring menacingly at the guilty parties. The craggy features of Pam's weather beaten face had proven particularly effective in this way on previous encounters with trespassers. Her piercing eyes, deeply inset above her cheekbones, blazed like blue-hot coals from her sockets. She was proud of this stare and the effect it usually had on unwelcome visitors. Often she had practiced it in front of the mirror in her bathroom. It had to be just right to achieve the intended effect.

This time it didn't work – its impact was lost on this group. Instead of sheepishly picking up their belongings and retreating to another part of the beach the tourists responded by taking pictures of the two old ladies. Shots were taken of the ladies lying down, sitting up, standing up and even going into their most threatening defensive postures. Insult was added to injury when one of the trespassers bowed to them and then asked Pam to take a picture of the group with one of their cameras. He handed his camera to her and the group posed by raising a toast to their day at the beach.

Pam was incensed!

Gesturing and cursing Pam flung the camera to the ground. Next she began to jump up and down on it with eyes blazing and nostrils flaring. The camera was beaten deeper and deeper into the sand as she continued with her enraged ritual.

The smiling and bowing ceased abruptly as the stunned tourists looked on in shocked disbelief.

In the meantime Alice had circled the group, ready to do battle if necessary to protect her beach as well as her friend. They were two tough old broads intent on securing their realm and they weren't planning to back down in any confrontation. By this time the attention of other inhabitants on the beach had focused on the disruption as they looked on in amusement.

"Go get 'em Alice!" shouted a laughing bystander – a regular at the beach.

Alice circled round and round like a wrestler feeling out an opponent. She crouched low to the ground ready to throw a tackle if need be. With the angle she assumed, her ample body threatened to topple her face first into the sand. Nevertheless her temples pulsated and her throat went dry as the excitement built toward a crescendo.

God was she glad for her training in self-defense as a prison guard!

Her expertise could come in handy here. Never mind that she was well past her prime and unlikely to be effectual in any possible altercation with the much younger party of tourists, she had a reputation to live up to and knew she could always fall back on her ability to deliver verbal abuse with the best of them.

By this time the tourists had recovered from their shock. The camera owner shook it vigorously to rid it of sand and began to launch a barrage of threatening words and gestures directed at the old ladies.

In the meantime Pam had picked up a bucket with sea water in it, ready to fling it at the bewildered party then run if necessary.

Just as the tension hit a high note the beach patrol arrived. It consisted of a single little Hawaiian man, with a frown on his face and a big whistle dangling from his neck.

In his job he walked frenetically up and down the beach all day long, looking for sun worshippers engaged in dangerous horseplay or drinking alcoholic beverages on the beach. He took particular delight when he found hidden liquor and beer containers protruding from under towels or from the inner depths of beach bags. Once he discovered an infringement he would gesture, stare, and shout at the guilty party until either the illegal activity ceased or the liquor was dumped in a garbage container. If this tactic didn't work his next move was to blow his whistle until it attracted the attention of a member of the Waikiki police force.

Upon his arrival at the scene he heard the screams and threats from the group of angry beachgoers as they prepared to do battle. His experienced eye quickly settled on the opened bottles of liquor lying on the blankets. A sniff of the glasses held by the tourists confirmed his suspicions.

To hell with this fracas, he thought, *there was a liquor infraction on his beach*. Now he could turn his attention to a more serious matter. With frenzied gestures and toots on his whistle he hustled the intruders off the beach to the delight and unadmitted relief of Pam and Alice.

As the morning wore on the sun's rays increased in intensity. Bud began to feel a warmth on his back which, if left unattended, would turn red and be a major discomfort later in the day. After all it was his first day at the beach and the generous layers of suntan lotion rubbed on his white body were no match for the tropical sun.

In the meantime, Ben, who had left his bench earlier to lie on the beach for a brief period of time, had beaten a hasty retreat back to his shady vantage point. He was acutely aware of the sun's intensity.

"Let's go back to the condo before I build a beet red tan like that idiot over there!" Bud yelled at Tina.

"Wait'll we go in for a quick dip," Tina responded.

She and Janice entered the shallow section of the salt water pool clutching their special beach gear. Given a depth of less than two feet and no waves, the women immediately took full command, though neither could swim a stroke. They held court without venturing deeper than their knees. The gear they put all their faith in were simply inflatable plastic surfboards purchased at an ABC store for less than two dollars. After returning from the dangers of the pool, Tina and Janice insisted on touching base with Terri and Mia before retreating back to the condos.

"So what's new?" Tina greeted Terri and Mia.

"Well, welcome back to Hawaii for one thing," Terri replied. "I see the old ladies still allow you on their part of the beach. They're getting more eccentric each year you know."

Terri's dislike of the old women was obvious. She knew about their backgrounds and had observed their outrageous and bizarre behavior and kept away from them.

One time, for example, the old ladies came to the beach drunk. Their excuse when Terri complained was that it had been Pam's birthday and she should butt out since they had the right to celebrate any way they wanted to. As an active member of her church back in Iowa, Terri had preached against loose morals and drinking. She also brought her six children up to strictly observe each of the Ten Commandments. However, in spite of her orthodox standards, Terri had a weakness for gossip and took a genuine liking to the outspoken natures of Tina and Janice.

"Why don't you ask Mia what's new?" Terri added.

"Why don't you piss off?" Mia echoed.

"Okay, Mia, what's new?"

"I don't want to talk about it."

"Aw come on. You can tell Janice and me. You know we always keep a secret."

"Sure you do. Oh, what the hell, the rest of the beach knows anyway. You see this expensive bathing suit I'm wearing? It cost 87 bucks. First of all, after paying that kind of money for an original designer suit, I found every second person wearing the damn thing. If that weren't enough I went body surfing the other day. Guess what? I floated around out there waiting for the big one. When it came I jumped on for the ride... Christ it was humungous! Just before I hit the beach it picked me up and flipped me upside down like a rag doll. When I stood up I was no longer wearing the bloody bathing suit."

"You should've seen it," Terri piped in, a smile lighting up her face. "The wave hit the beach with a huge crash. It was one of the biggest I've seen here in some time. Amid all the white froth and debris I spotted what looked like a piece of green seaweed. When I looked over at Mia I could see her hugging the sand, face down. As soon as I realized that the green seaweed was actually her new bathing suit I went over and got it for her. You should have seen the quick change that took place when I gave it back. She wriggled face down in the sand into her suit. I still don't know how she did it, hugging the sand so tightly like that."

"Yeah, well you would have too. And those old women friends of yours just pointed and laughed. They were a hell of a lot closer to it than Terri was."

Mia hadn't returned to the beach for the next three days. She was too embarrassed to show her face. Shortly after, however, she regained her composure. Besides, a new crop of tourists were now on the beach and they wouldn't have witnessed her most embarrassing moment.

"Hey, that's funny Mia. Bet you can't do it again," Bud teased. He had overheard the story.

"Up yours, Bud," Mia shot back.

"Mind your own business, Bud. She wasn't telling you the story. You're a pain in the ass," Tina added to the tirade.

At this point Bud held his tongue and just grinned at the thought of Mia hugging the sand while her bathing suit swirled in the surf.

"Well, Mia, see you later at the pub. We're going back to the condo to change." With a flip of her head and Bud in tow, Tina set out for their suite.

CHAPTER 4

The Melting Pot

B ud peered through the doorway of the pub and into the dark inner recesses of the bar. His figure, framed in the doorway, formed a link between the brightness outside and the darkness within. Viewed from inside the room a bright halo formed around his profile.

As his eyes slowly adjusted to the pitch-blackness of the room, the general shape of figures emerged. Soon he was able to make out the silhouettes of two couples at a table near the front, the usual complement of bar flies sitting on stools at the bar, and several groups of imbibers at tables scattered throughout the rest of the room. Slowly familiar objects became recognizable and the features of patrons took form. He slammed the door on the brilliant sunshine and entered, engulfed by the darkness within.

"Hey snowbird, I see yer back fer 'nother round of paradise!" a familiar voice shot out from the vicinity of the bar.

There was no mistaking that voice. Its gravelly quality boomed from the inner sanctum of the darkened room. It carried with it the promise of far fetched stories and of profanities yet to be uttered. The Admiral was leaning against the bar with his hand fondling the thigh of a disheveled redhead who was completely oblivious to his probing fingers working their way closer and closer toward their final destination.

"Well if it isn't the skipper himself. I see you're up to your usual tricks," Bud replied.

"Have a drink on me mate! Make it a Blue Hawaii t'go with yer white ass an' red nose. Then ya can pretend yer the national flag," the Admiral quipped, looking noticeably pleased with his wit.

Bud sidled up to the bar next to the old man. He placed his hand, like a catcher's mitt, on the top of the bar waiting for Rita the barmaid to slide a drink the length of it.

"Hey red white and blue. Bud this Bud's for you!" Rita called out. She was pleased with herself for coming up with something related to the Admiral's wisecrack. "This one's on the house. Your first of the season."

A beer slid the length of the bar.

"Thanks Rita you're a honey. Some day we've got to get it on."

It wasn't a Mai Tai but it would be an adequate replacement to quench the insatiable thirst he had generated on his walk from the condo.

* * * * * * *

The bar flies weren't the only thing that made the Melting Pot such an interesting and pleasurable place to spend time – it was also the music. The pub featured local musicians who entertained the clientele each afternoon and evening. Most of the entertainers were Hawaiians who demonstrated great talent with musical instruments and possessed wonderful voices. They also had great senses of humor, interacting exceptionally well with the audiences.

One of the favorite acts was a wife and husband team named Sally and Bally. Sally was a gorgeous lady who sang beautifully, like an exquisite songbird. Bally, on the other hand, had a passable voice but played the guitar exceptionally well. His sense of humor, however, was somewhat bizarre. He often wore a baseball cap with the words "**Don't piss me off**" embroidered on the outside peak. If a patron gave him a hard time he would bow in the direction of the critic and point to the words on the outside peak of the hat. Once he gained the attention of the heckler he would flip the peak up and reveal the following additional words: "**You're a fuckin' jerk!**" This routine was wildly received by the rest of the customers and they would try to provoke him, in a good natured way, to become the next recipient of Bally's "brush off".

The routine became so popular that eventually he had hundreds of these hats produced to sell to eager customers. Tina purchased four as props for her gossip sessions back in Seattle.

* * * * * *

Bud glanced carefully around the room drinking in familiar sights and nodding knowingly to the regulars who frequented the establishment. Through the corner of one eye he could still make out the Admiral talking a blue streak as his hand continued its expedition with the redhead.

Reflections on the Admiral

The Admiral was a regular patron of the Melting Pot, spending every waking moment at the bar. Once settled he only left his stool when a potential female victim, sitting alone at one of the tables, caught his eye, or when he had to go to the can.

He was a big man, more than six feet tall and weighed about two hundred and fifty pounds. A skipper's hat trimmed with gold braid was always perched jauntily on his head. His neatly trimmed beard, laced with silver, gave him a distinguished appearance which helped to charm the ladies. His dapper appearance and apparent sex drive belied his age of approximately 70 years.

None of the patrons or employees of the bar knew for sure where the Admiral originally came from. They weren't even sure whether he really had been a seaman in his earlier life. Rumors of his past included everything from being captain of a deep sea freighter to a farmer from the Midwest who had never been to sea. The Admiral gave the appearance of a seaman but never spoke of the details of his life before his arrival at the Melting Pot. An incident two years earlier, however, cast some doubt about the likelihood he had a seafaring past.

In this instance the Admiral successfully picked up a lady tourist from Arizona by the name of Rose who had never been on a ship before. She talked him into taking her on one of the dinner cruises which plied the waters off Waikiki's shoreline. In an attempt to impress her, the Admiral talked at length about nautical topics during the two or three days preceding the date of sail. He became almost insufferable to the other patrons of the bar as seafaring terms were worked into every topic of conversation. His reference to the can became the "head", the front of the bar the "bow", behind the bar the "foc'sle", and the rear of the bar the "stern".

"Hey sweets, smile at the cap'n now! That's right, a big smile. Keep it up an we'll pipe you on deck as the bo'sun's mate when we set sail next week." The Admiral clicked the camera and it captured Rose's big smile.

"Oh Addie," Rose fawned. "You know so much about the sea. I can hardly wait to cruise with my very own admiral."

A sheepish grin wrestled with the rough and ready features of his face. He flashed a quick smile at his lady friend and laid the camera on the bar.

"Awright ever'one let's drink up b'fore we set sail," he bellowed.

The Admiral continued to take every opportunity to coin a salty phrase in an attempt to impress his new girlfriend. By the time the day of embarkation finally arrived the bar's inhabitants were fed up. He had become a real pain in the ass.

As the story went, the Admiral continued to banter about life at sea as he and Rose walked on board the small cruise ship. They walked arm in arm with Rose's uplifted eyes full of admiration as she gazed at her special man in uniform. Once on board it soon became embarrassing for Rose when the Admiral proceeded to hound the skipper of the vessel as if he were the man in charge. He wanted to know compass directions for the planned course, the estimated time of arrival back on the dock, the tide changes, the wind direction and whether or not the boat had radar and sonar. Hell, the boat was only seventy feet long and never left sight of the shore line during its brief nightly run of only two hours.

The vessel's skipper soon tired of this blowhard and wanted to get rid of him. After managing to ease him from the bridge the boat finally cast off from the dock.

"Christ," the skipper of the vessel muttered under his breath. "These bloody know it all tourists are getting worse."

The Admiral worked his way back to the holding area, conscious of glances from fellow passengers which he interpreted as perceptions that he was skipper of the boat – likely due to the sea captain's cap which he wore cockily on his head.

While the boat was still in the calm of the harbor, the Admiral began with his stories of the sea and its storms and how he had survived the worst it had to offer. Soon a cluster of passengers formed around him as he used his charm, wit, and rough and ready manner to add credibility to the yarns.

When the boat finally left the confines of the harbor the chopping movement of the open sea embraced the structure in a vice-like grip. As it turned into the waves a rhythmic motion took over. The ship continued with an up and down motion as it plied its way through the open waters. After clearing the shallow water a gentler up and down motion greeted the vessel and the passengers were lulled into a sense of complacency. After all the shore was still in sight and they felt safe with the experienced Admiral in charge of the boat. He was a man who took the time to meet with them and to tell stories of his earlier exploits. A man who had encountered and conquered the worst the sea had to offer.

After less than ten minutes in the rocking motion of the open sea the Admiral's stories began to lose their zeal – almost as if he were running out of words to share with the passengers. He began speaking slowly and less audibly. His lips began to quiver and a look of gravity formed on his face as he stopped, mid-sentence, during a story.

"Excuse me, I haf't' get back to m'bridge," he announced to the crowd as he hurried off.

Several of the passengers commented on how it must have been important for him to take the wheel in these changeable waters. But Rose thought it strange that he was heading in the direction opposite to the bridge.

The Admiral was nowhere to be seen for the rest of the two hour trip. Rose searched everywhere. First she thought he must be busy bothering the crew. However, after a half hour she became annoyed. The first place she checked was the other passenger lounge in case he was telling stories again. He wasn't there. Next she headed toward the bridge in case he was with the ship's captain.

That's the trouble, she thought. *When a man re-visits an activity in which he had spent his lifetime he's liable to be swapping stories with other professionals still involved in it.*

But he wasn't there.

Next, anger took over. Imagine being asked on a date and then getting stood up while still on it. After another half hour with no Admiral in sight her anger turned to worry. What if he fell overboard? Should she tell a crew member? No, he was too experienced a seaman for that to happen. Finally she went to report his disappearance to a crew member.

"**Man overboard! Man overboard**!" the PA system bellowed. The boat began a wide circle and then retraced its steps on the way back to the harbor.

"When did you see him last? What direction was he going in? What did he say?"

All of the questions upset Rose even more. When it came down to it she really didn't know him that well.

"Was he depressed? Did he ever talk about suicide?"

God! It was a nightmare. Imagine if her date resulted in a death; why did this have to happen to her? Rose had grown almost hysterical by this time. The questions kept coming and she didn't know how to answer them. Finally she burst into tears, her body throbbing with emotion. Sobbing, she told them to buggar off and leave her alone.

After what seemed like an eternity in hell the boat finally reached the dock. The police were waiting as the shore lines were thrown on the dock and tied onto the large metal cleats to secure the boat. The other passengers disembarked and Rose was left standing alone by the gangplank.

The police were talking to the captain of the vessel. Suddenly the captain turned to face Rose's direction and a large policeman called her over.

"Awright miss, what's yer name?"

"R-r-r-r-rose!" she stuttered.

"An yer missing boyfriend, what's his name?"

"A-d-d-d-d-d-d-mir'l", came the response

"Lis'n honey, I don' mean his rank or job, what's his real name?"

"I j-j-j-j-j-ust called him Addie. Y' know, short for Admiral. He kinda liked it when I called him that. But nobody else dared t'call him that name," she blubbered.

"That don' tell me much. Awright what happened? When did ya see him last? What'd he say? What direction was he goin' in? Was he depressed? Did he ever talk 'bout suicide?" They were the same set of questions once again.

Rose's body went numb; she was in a state of shock as the questions came fast and furious. They were almost identical to the ones she answered while still on the boat. By the time they finished Rose was reduced to a pile of raw nerves. Her body shook and her eyes were red and swollen from crying.

Suddenly the forlorn figure of a man stumbled out of the washroom and onto the deck. A white cap sat askew on his head. His face was ashen, the color of white chalk, and he lurched along the deck with an unsteady gait. His eyes, the color of fiery red coals, darted left and right as he made his way toward the gangplank. Suddenly he looked upward and his gaze met the gathering up on the dock. Quickly he slunk behind a lifeboat, trying to hide from the group.

"Look! Look! Someone's still on the boat," a voice from the dock cried out.

It was the Admiral!

He had spent the remainder of the trip hiding in the can, seasick beyond belief. This so-called experienced seaman who claimed to have taken the best the sea could offer couldn't handle the sea's gentle movement on a dinner cruise. In just moments Rose experienced a wide range of emotions: a tremendous sense of relief, anger at this fraudulent seaman who had put her through such a traumatic experience, pity for him and finally, a sense of joy as the humor of the situation struck her. The latter emotion won out as she thought of how this phony and comical character had received his just deserts. A mischievous smile formed on her lips; she could hardly wait to tell everyone back at the bar.

The Admiral wasn't present when Rose announced the news to the bar patrons. She took great delight in dwelling on his poor sea legs. Weeks passed before he re-established his daily routine on the barstool. By this time Rose had returned to Arizona and the incident was all but forgotten by the remaining bar flies.

In spite of his unprincipled ways the community of misfits liked the Admiral. A special sense of belonging was shared among all of them. They shared a relationship similar to that of family ... but at arms length. Bud recalled an incident the previous year when they all shared a common concern about the old man's health.

* * * * * * * * * * *

A relationship the Admiral established with one of the young ladies he picked up had grown to have special meaning for him. She was a beautiful girl with long sensuous legs, a tiny waist and breasts that threatened to erupt from the confines of her enormous bra. No one was sure what drew her to him. She was 40 years his junior and could have had her pick of any young stud she wanted. Perhaps it was his wit and charm or a suspicion that he had money. The relationship continued to grow more serious until one day the Admiral announced he and the sweet young thing were going to be married.

The bar flies couldn't believe their ears! They had cause to worry since the Admiral had a history of heart problems and the thought of him keeping up with this young sex pot gave cause for concern. Rita the barmaid brought it to his attention.

"You know Admiral; you're biting off more than you can chew. You have a heart condition and she's so young and sexy. When you screw her it could result in death."

"Well, if she dies, she dies!" the Admiral roared nonchalantly.

As it turned out the expectant bride left the sinking ship before the wedding. The young lady had found out that the Admiral was not a rich man after all. She disappeared with greater haste than she had arrived.

Brad the Bar Fly

Sitting next to the Admiral at the bar was Brad, a bespeckled little man who left the frigid and windswept city of Chicago behind at this time every year. Back home he was a bookkeeper who enjoyed numbers more than people. Immediately upon his arrival each year in Waikiki he hurried to the Melting Pot before his bags were even unpacked. He never went to the beach for a walk or to a restaurant. His entire life, while on vacation, revolved around his bar stool.

All of Brad's waking hours in Waikiki were spent at the bar drinking booze and eating pupus; the snacks served with drinks in Hawaiian bars. He seldom spoke to anyone. Slight nods of the head or a shrug of the shoulders were usually the extent of his conversation. He just sat on his barstool emitting the odd grunt when someone directed a question his way. Brad seldom joined in the hijinks that others engaged in at the bar. Although he was not an outgoing participant he still subscribed to the nebulous bond shared among the inhabitants.

Next to Brad sat Mia. She always sat on the same stool, claiming ownership in a way similar to Pam and Alice's annexation of their section of beach. All of the regulars knew of Mia's fondness for that seat. In fact Rita had attached a sign to it that read *Mia's Place*.

When Brad first visited the bar he wasn't aware of the significance of the sign as he slid onto the stool to order a drink. He was lost in thought, sipping his drink when Mia arrived.

"Hey, you! Can't you read?"

Brad ignored the question as he attempted to shrug and grunt his way out of the confrontation. He hated violence of any type and was completely oblivious of the cause of the sharp question directed his way. His next strategy was to add a silly looking grin from his repertoire of responses.

"Get the hell off my seat before I wipe that stupid grin off your face!"

Brad moved like lightning. He had got the message. It was fortunate for him that he moved so quickly since Mia had been a martial arts expert in her younger days. Some of the bar patrons still remembered the time that a tough looking biker ignored her demand to move and promptly found himself on his ass, with Mia standing over him, posed in a karate stance.

"S-s-sorry about that M-m-maa'm," Brad stammered a reply.

"Don't worry, be happy you little fart. Besides you can buy me a drink," she replied with sudden good humor.

After that episode Brad and Mia became friends. Actually Mia was a favorite of most of the patrons, in particular Rita and the Admiral. Rita liked her because she could keep unruly customers in line and the Admiral admired her for her prowess. Actually the only patron Mia didn't get along with was Rocco. They hated each other vehemently. Both knew acquaintances from the underworld and, on occasion, had threatened each other through those contacts. This intense dislike of Rocco was shared by the Admiral.

Bill the Bar Fly

Next to Mia sat Bill and Sue Jackson from California. Bill was a mathematics teacher in the Los Angeles school system and his wife was a secretary at one of the schools. Their annual visit to Hawaii at this time of year was always short since it had to coincide with the time schools were closed for the Christmas holiday season. Bill always drank himself into a stupor before the evening was over. He claimed it was his way of hanging loose and forgetting "them little bastards who have no appreciation for the beauty of the quadratic formula."

Bill was muttering incoherently as Sue tried to pry him from his stool so she could guide him back to their hotel room.

"Algebra is good for ever'body. Those lil' sons of bitches don't know what's good fr'em," he muttered.

Sue managed to get him off the stool and pointed toward the doorway. They made their exit with Bill still muttering along the way.

* * * * * *

"Bud where'n hells yer crew?" the Admiral demanded gruffly.

"Tina and Janice are out shopping and Ben's nursing his sunburn. The women will be here any minute though."

"What makes ya so sure? I know they spend hours in them shops an blow most o' the money ya bring over."

"I'm positive they'll be here any minute. Let's see, they've been gone now for about 45 minutes."

"Bullshit! They won't even be warmed up. They'll be gone fer hours. What makes ya such a smart ass t'know they'll be here any minute?"

"I know because the credit card I gave Tina expired last month," he replied glibly. With this announcement Bud smiled at the other bar patrons. He turned a full 360 degrees while taking a sweeping bow, pleased with his trick on Tina.

Just then Ben appeared in the doorway wearing an incandescent glow and reeking of sunburn lotion. He painstakingly made his way over to the bar and perched on the stool next to Bud.

"Have any of you seen Rocco?" Ben asked the group.

No response.

Rocco hadn't been seen for days. In fact the last time he appeared at the bar was more than a week ago. At that time he had cautiously entered the room, looked nervously from side to side, eyes darting about the extremities, and then abruptly departed.

Not hearing a response to his question Ben settled into his drink. At that point the front door burst open and Tina and Janice stormed into the bar.

"You asshole!" Tina shouted.

"Yeah you're an asshole!" Janice echoed.

"Ben the women are calling Rocco names again and he's not even here," Bud called out. "Admiral tell the ladies they need an appointment if they want to talk to Rocco."

The Admiral decided to take a rain check on Bud's invitation. He had seen Tina and Janice in this mood once before. At that time they dumped all the drinks sitting on the bar over the heads and laps of everyone nearby. Ben, unaware of the credit card episode, tried to calm them down.

Why don't you toot off in your tug!" Janice yelled back at him. "And take Bud and the Admiral with you."

Eventually the women settled down and joined the rest of them for a drink. As the afternoon wore on the Whites and Toppers actively planned for dinner and the rest of the evening.

The Arrival of Rocco

Rocco emerged from the craps game with the cockiness of a big cat about to pounce on a cornered prey. His chest was pumped and his hips held a swagger that belied his short stature. He was a big winner – the last toss of the dice had been worth a cool 10 grand. What a throw, he beamed to himself, unwilling to credit the loaded dice that he had slipped into his hand. The suckers had been too dumb to notice it. Now he would go to the Melting Pot and show everyone how important he was.

With a smile on his face and twenty dollar bills protruding from his pockets, Rocco sauntered through the door and into the Melting Pot, his image adsorbed by the darkness within. *God*, he thought, am *I going to make a big splash with the waitresses and bar flies.*

"Hi y'all! Rocco's back and I'm loaded!"

He yanked a bill from his shirt pocket and stuffed it down Rita's blouse. She giggled and said, "That felt good Rocco, do it again." Whereupon he grabbed five more bills and deposited them in the same location.

"Drinks for the house – make'm all doubles!" he roared with a big grin on his face. *This is showin' them how important I am*, he thought to himself. Now everyone would like him. He went from table to table, dropping bills in front of each of the women.

In the background Tina grimaced as the spectacle continued. *What an asshole*, she thought. Finally he arrived at the table where the two Seattle couples sat.

"Hi Ben old buddy. Share some of this stuff with me." He dropped a wad of money on the table in front of Ben. "And Janice, there's plenty more of this stuff for you."

"Hi Bud," he acknowledged, going around the table. Rocco hesitated before approaching Tina. "Well my little Tina. What can I do for you? Your wish is my command."

"You can fuck off!" cracked the response. Tina abruptly flung herself from the chair and stomped out of the bar followed by Bud, Janice and Ben.

Rocco just shrugged his shoulders and proceeded over to the bandstand. "Hey Bally, guess what I've got for Sally." He gave her another wad of bills, careful not to try stuffing them down her blouse since Bally had a mean temper and was fast with his fists.

Suddenly Rocco felt a pair of piercing eyes trained directly on him. He froze – then abruptly ran out of the bar.

Little did Rocco know that his life was about to become hell.

Chapter 5

Rocco

Rocco muttered to himself as he rushed along the crowded street. *Goddamn idiots! I told them not to pass the take without checking first. Did they check? No! The assholes didn't check. Now I'm in for it. The goddamn assholes!*

His head throbbed with pain as the bright sunlight pierced his eyes. Its brilliance bore right through to the sockets. The only way he could maneuver was by shielding his eyes with one hand while focusing his line of sight on the sidewalk. The constant churning in his gut kept him on the verge of nausea. He was almost doubled over pressing his stomach in an effort to compensate for the pain. With one hand over his eyes and the other pushed against his midsection he cut an ungainly figure as he stumbled down the street.

Soon Rocco began to pick up speed – darting between people in the throng, picking holes, flowing against the grain of movement like a halfback working his way downfield. However his clumsy gait was far from the fluid movement of a running back in flight. He jostled against several pedestrians who stopped to stare after the bumbling figure.

"Up yours!" an exasperated hooker screamed as he brushed against her body in his rush to nowhere.

It was a good thing he had detected The Man's piercing eyes when he glanced toward the darkness at the back of the pub. He thought he had got out before one of the henchmen was alerted but couldn't be sure. Now he had to make tracks before someone was on his tail.

It had been over a week since he first heard that a contract was out on his life. During that time Rocco had not returned to his home in the valley and avoided frequenting his usual spots. He had, however, returned briefly to his favorite hang out, the Melting Pot, once or twice. Nothing he had seen suggested that a paid killer lurked.

But the word was out on the street just the same!

He had checked with Rita the barmaid at the Melting Pot to find out whether anyone had asked questions about him and drew a blank. She hadn't noticed any suspicious characters hanging around the bar, but with all the tourists in town it was difficult to spot a potential hit man. Besides Rocco didn't trust any of the regulars at the bar since few, if any, liked him and the hit man could easily be one of them.

Rocco broke into a cold sweat as he thought about Sid, one of his cousins. Sid tried to hold back some collection money from The Man and for a while lived like a king – throwing money around on girls and booze. It wasn't long before word reached The Man whose reward to Sid was a pair of cement boots. They found him in about 30 feet of water. By the time the rock crabs and fish had finished there wasn't much left – just shreds of clothing and bones protruding from a concrete base.

Damn! How can I get off this island without The Man knowing?

The Man had contacts on the docks and at the airport. It was unlikely Rocco could slip through without being noticed. His portly frame and Bronx accent gained attention wherever he went. His mind flashed back to the events of last week when he had agreed to the rake off and to split the proceeds from the floating crap game. He planned to tell The Man that one of the suckers from the mainland hit it big on the last roll. He shouldn't have listened to that yahoo from the mainland, allowing cooked dice to be exchanged for those used by the house. The plan was to meet the con man the next morning for the split. But the mainlander never showed up. Now Rocco was a sucker twice over; he didn't get his share of the sting and The Man was onto his game.

Only a year ago Rocco had held a steady job driving a tow motor in the packing plant and picking up a few extra bucks bootlegging on the side. After Sid's disappearance he was offered a job by The Man. He'd jumped at it! It would give him the bucks needed to live a flashy lifestyle and to impress his friends.

Rocco was basically insecure and badly needed people to like him. In order to solicit friends he squandered all of his money on them. Barmaids and cocktail waitresses were showered with gifts. He even took out a loan on his flashy convertible one Christmas for money to lavish expensive presents on the girls. They tolerated him for his extravagant generosity. Others, like Mia and the Admiral, despised him.

In Mia's case, she could clearly see through Rocco's façade. It was obvious to her that not only was his extravagant generosity a cover up for insecurity, but also an element of cruelness was evident by some of his actions. Mia recalled that when one of his girlfriends complained about gifts going to other girls, she saw Rocco backhand both sides of her face. Then he'd laughed as blood spurted out of her nose and down her blouse.

Although the Admiral initially tolerated Rocco he quickly changed his opinion when he caught Rocco palming a card during a high stakes poker game. The Admiral, who had been easygoing and gregarious until then, grabbed Rocco by the shirt and yanked him right over the table. As Rocco attempted to retaliate the Admiral yanked a knife from the inside of one of his boots and threatened to castrate him.

"Get your ass out of here, you goddamn cheat before you lose your manhood!" bellowed the Admiral.

Humiliated, Rocco beat a hasty retreat. As he ran out the door he swore to himself that he would get even.

* * * * * * * *

Rocco's Earlier Years

Rocco's insecurity was due, in part, to an unhappy childhood. He was born to Richard and Mindy Drinke, on March 8, 1945, in the bedroom of a run down flat located in the Upper Bronx. He was named Richard Junior after his father. As he grew into adulthood, however, the name he became most accustomed to was either Dick or Dickie. This convention caused him considerable unhappiness as he progressed though his school years.

His father, Richard Drinke, was a plumber by trade. He was a heavy drinker and often got into brawls in the taverns he frequented. On occasion he returned home drunk after a night on the town and abused his wife both verbally and physically. Mindy put up with this routine for the first two years of marriage but threatened to leave her husband if it continued. As is turned out she was about to make good on it.

The Second World War had ended two months after Richard Junior's birth and veterans, recently returned from overseas, flooded the streets and nightclubs of New York. While her husband was out drinking Mindy began sneaking out to nightclubs to dance. She left Richard Junior with one of her neighbors to babysit whenever she went out on one of these escapades.

Her baby was less than six months old when Mindy took up with a returned service man and disappeared, never to be seen again by her husband or son. At this tender age the baby was packed up and sent off to be raised by his paternal grandmother; a lady who considered this to be an imposition of considerable magnitude and who, throughout the days of Richard's youth, barely tolerated him.

Richard Junior was not popular with other children either. They made fun of him and refused to play with him. The outlandish clothes his grandmother dressed him in did not help. He was forced to wear short pants, plaid shirts and suspenders throughout his elementary school years. In those days that attire was considered square. He became a target for practical jokes and was never selected when teams were picked for sports. As a result he became a loner who seldom spoke either in class or at play.

He became the nerd of Roosevelt Elementary school and it wasn't long before Dicky Drinke became Dick the Dink.

"Dick the Dink! Dick the Dink! He wears short pants and his feet stink!" taunted the kids on the playground.

Richard Junior seethed in humiliation as this slogan took the playground by storm. He swore to himself that someday he would show all of them. They would cower at his feet when he became rich and powerful. To compensate Richard daydreamed a lot. His fantasies usually revolved around events of fame and fortune. As he grew older he added sex to the screenplay.

Richard never finished high school. He couldn't concentrate on studies, was not good at sports and his unpopularity denied him the social perks that went with school. He decided to go out into the world to make lots of money. He dreamt of a triumphant return to school a year later, driving a shiny red Cadillac convertible. In his mind his popularity would be immediate as girls swooned over the car and grasped at the twenty dollar bills he planned to wave in their faces.

His first job was as a door to door salesman with Fuller Brush. That job lasted two days. After dozens of doors slammed in his face all he had to show for his efforts were sore feet and the sale of one tin of shoe polish. Next, he tried Amway. That didn't work either. Dreams of a triumphant return to school quickly disappeared.

Eventually he landed a job clearing tables at a local restaurant. It wasn't good money but at least it provided him with a measure of independence from his domineering grandmother. While working at this job he had his first date with a girl. It was with one of the waitresses who had felt sorry for him and took him under her wing. Their relationship grew until he experienced, at first hand and for the first time, the real differences between men and women.

Her name was Dianne. She was two years older than Richard and a recent arrival to the city. She had left her hometown in Iowa against the wishes of her parents, intent on becoming a model in the big city of New York. To date she had been offered only one modeling job. It turned out to be a nude layout for one of the skin magazines. She turned that offer down since she had no intention of taking off her clothes in front of a camera. The photographer had sneered at her as she left his studio her modesty intact.

"Just wait, baby you'll crawl back, begging to do a buff scene when you're hungry enough. You ain't got nothing special you know!"

Shaken by this experience Dianne considered returning home to Iowa. However, shortly afterward she noticed a "waitress wanted" sign in the window of a restaurant and here she was.

Dianne had been working in the restaurant for about one month when she noticed a rather pathetic looking kid walk in to ask the manager for a job. She felt sorry for him as he mumbled his request to the boss. The manager must have felt some empathy as well since Richard was given a job clearing tables and washing dishes – even though no job was vacant at the time. It wasn't long before she grew to like the shy young kid. Eventually she issued an invitation to dinner in her apartment and a sexual relationship ensued. She was rather amused at how naive and inexperienced he was. He had never even kissed a girl before let alone made love.

Richard, however, proved to be an adept student who learned much more about life in one short week in Dianne's bed than he had during the previous year at school.

"Don't be so square, Richard. This can be fun if you just relax." Her hand encircled his manhood, ready to begin the experiment. "Why don't I call you Ricky. Is that all right Ricky?"

"Why not? It's better than Dickie."

"God, you're still hard as a rock... Hey! we should call you Rocco."

"Why not? Call me Rocco the Rock."

Rocco became the name that Richard would respond to for the rest of his life. He liked it. It conveyed a macho image and helped him to get over the unpleasant memories of his earlier life as a wimp.

Armed with a new name, newfound experience as a man, and a more confident outlook on life, Rocco was ready to conquer the world. He tried a number of get-rich-quick deals during the next several years. Among them: selling shares in illegal pyramid schemes, hawking wares at carnivals and bootlegging moonshine. His efforts met with mixed success. Whenever he made a buck he blew it – usually to impress people or in an attempt to buy friends. It was his lack of acceptance during his earlier school days that caused his continual quest for popularity.

Eventually Rocco ended up in Honolulu. After several stints as a waiter and one as a real estate agent he settled down for a short while as a tow motor driver in a warehouse. That job ended abruptly when he ran over the foreman's foot while backing up with a load of pallet boards on the forks of the tow motor.

He continued to blow his money in an attempt to become popular and was always on the lookout for ways to make easy money on the side.

In the meantime Rocco continued to gravitate from one bar to the next looking for companionship and for others to impress. One day he arrived at the front door of the Melting Pot and went in searching for a way to meet his needs. In order to gain attention he tipped the waitresses generously and bought the bar flies free drinks. He was accepted immediately and finally, he thought, he had found his new home. Suddenly he felt a strange sensation in the back of his head, as if someone were staring at him. Turning around he encountered a pair of piercing eyes inset in a finely chiseled face – staring directly at him. Then the eyes quickly turned away and the owner hurriedly darted out the back door of the bar.

"Who was that?" Rocco demanded of Rita the barmaid.

"That person visits here often but seldom talks to any of us. I think there might be a criminal element involved. I get a creepy feeling when those eyes take me in. We just call that character ***The Man***."

Rocco shrugged it off and continued giving everyone the impression he was a big shot. After a week his money began to run low. He needed to make more – and fast. Hearing that they may be hiring at the docks he went down to look for work. Any kind of work would do, legal or illegal, as long as it paid good bucks. He had heard that longshoremen made good money and hence his arrival at the waterfront. Looking around he could see a couple of tow motors carrying pallet boards, stacked high with boxes, from the dock to a warehouse in the back. Several men were operating winches, lifting containers from the deck of a ship up to the dock. Looking further, he could see groups of workers in various locations, lounging around and smoking cigarettes. Later he was to learn that these were back-up men for the tow motor drivers and winch operators. Rocco thought that was a soft touch made just for him and he immediately planned to land one of the jobs. First, he eased his way over to a group of men to ask how to get a job on the docks. A couple of them just shrugged and ignored him but one of the older ones told him to go to the union hiring hall. He asked directions and then proceeded toward that location. Once there, he went up to a desk and asked how to sign up for work.

"Well mate, ya need to fill in this form and then drop it off at the counter over there."

Rocco quickly filled in the form and took it over to the counter with the sign "Applications for Work" on it.

"When do I start work?" Rocco asked the clerk behind the counter.

"Who knows? Maybe today, maybe tomorrow, maybe never."

"What'd you mean?"

"You'll be on the *Spare Board*. Show up here early tomorrow morning and there may be work or there may not be. It depends how many ships are here to unload and how many of our regulars show up to work."

Rocco showed up early the next morning and hung around with a dozen other *Spare Boarders*. There was no work for him that day. He repeated this routine for the next three days and still no work. Finally, on the fourth day he lucked out. With a slip of paper in his hand he reported for work to the foreman of the winch stations.

"You run one of these winches before?" the foreman questioned.

"Of course," Rocco lied. "I have six years experience on the docks in Seattle and San Francisco." He had falsely reported experience at operating winches and securing ships on his application form. Actually Rocco had never even set foot on a dock before.

"Awright. I'm not interested in your family history. Get your ass over to Number Three and start bringing up those containers from the hold."

Rocco went over to the winch and studied the buttons on the shaft. One said "Up" one said "Down" and another "Stop". Each of the up and down buttons could be adjusted for speed. *Hell*, Rocco thought, *this is a piece of cake.* He sauntered over to the winch, peered around and shrugged his shoulders. *This'll show 'em*, he thought. He could pretend to be an experienced operator with the best of them. *In no time I'll work myself up to foreman.*

"**Up on number three!**" a voice shouted from the ship's deck far below.

Rocco immediately sprung to action. *What a lark!* By mistake, he pushed the *down* button and the cable immediately went slack.

"**What the hell is going on up there?**" a voice shouted from below.

"**Dry up! I'm just checking the gear!**" he shot back.

Next, Rocco pushed the *up* button and the cable sprung to life. It tightened instantly and violently jerked the pallet board at the other end. A scrambling sound could be heard from the deck below.

"**Watch it you asshole**," a voice boomed from the deck of the ship.

Rocco ignored the protest and continued bringing the pallet board upwards. It swung wildly back and forth, going faster and faster. *How the hell do you slow this thing down?* Rocco thought in a panic. All of a sudden the load reached the top of the winch and with a crash it spilled the contents all over the dock.

"**What's going on? What's going on?**" the foreman screamed as he ran over to the winch.

"**Nothing**," Rocco retorted. "**Stuff it up your ass. Your goddamn equipment is broken**." With that response he threw off his work gloves and stomped off the dock. This was the end of Rocco's brief experience as a longshoreman.

But he needed a job and needed one bad.

* * * * * * * * * * * * * * *

Rocco migrated back to the Melting Pot – anxious to seek advice on money-making opportunities from the bar flies without putting his flamboyant reputation at risk. He was deeply concerned about his rapidly dwindling money supply but didn't want them to know.

"Any ideas where some big money can be made? I don't care if it's legal or not." He threw out the question in a rhetorical manner, not expecting any useful response.

"You could rob a bank," one of the drunks offered.

"No, that's illegal. Why don't you just collect all the debts everyone owes you?" a second offered. "That way you could just give it all back to everyone and we would all be happy."

This bantering of useless ideas continued as Rocco sat in deep thought. Once again he felt the strange sensation on the back of his head that he had experienced before. It felt as if someone was staring at him intently. He quickly turned his head and observed a pair of piercing eyes studying him – like liquid lava they burned through to his soul. This time the eyes remained trained on its target. It was The Man.

A crooked finger suddenly appeared and Rocco was beckoned over to his side.

"Can you keep a secret?" The Man demanded of Rocco. "I need someone who can keep secrets and who has no fear of the law. Can you use a gun?"

"Y-y-yeesss," Rocco stammered.

"Good. I've been watching you for the last couple of weeks and you may be the person I'm looking for. I need someone to run numbers for me and to drive my clients to secret gambling locations and illegal cockfights."

"I'm your guy," Rocco replied. "Is the pay good?"

"How does 2000 bucks a week plus commissions sound?"

"Fantastic!"

Rocco began working for The Man the next day. He was given a fancy limousine to drive while on duty – which turned out to be 24 hours a day. One of his jobs was to pick up high rollers at the airport from the other islands and the mainland and drive them and their girlfriends to a swank hotel. When the gambling and cock fights were scheduled he drove them to the secret location. It changed frequently and he never knew until the last minute where to go. While the illegal activities were taking place Rocco was given a gun and told to stand watch for any cars approaching the secluded area. He was to stop these cars, tell them they were on private property, and to get the hell off. If it was the cops he was to remain hidden and fire in the air three times. This would alert the gamblers so that incriminating evidence could be hidden or destroyed.

His other main job was to run numbers. He would collect the bets and pay off the winners. When there was a big payout a big production was made. It drew the attention of all the fellow workers of the big winner and usually resulted in more numbers being played the next time.

This routine was ideal for Rocco. He made big bucks, had an exciting lifestyle and the means to try to impress all of his friends and acquaintances.

* * * * * * * * *

It was during this period of his life that Rocco first met the snowbirds. He was drawn to them by their kibitzing and friendly manner. He envied their close friendships and badly wanted to be part of the group. To facilitate this need to belong he attempted to shower them with gifts and to buy all of their drinks. However this was met with resistance as the others insisted on paying their share. It was a unique experience for Rocco who expected everyone to accept his generosity with no questions asked. However he continued to actively seek their companionship and eventually developed a friendship with Ben.

Rocco was drawn to Ben because of the deals the tugboat skipper always talked about. Stories of the unfinished marina and the soon to be planned apartment complex fascinated Rocco. He was convinced Ben was going to hit it big and he wanted to go along for the ride.

When the chance to work for The Man had presented itself Rocco jumped at it. After all, he would have more money than ever before and be able to buy the gratitude of the friends he so desperately sought. It didn't matter that the work involved illegal gambling and the numbers game since Rocco had already cut his teeth on bootlegging and on several unsuccessful attempts at pimping. As long as there was no violence he was all for it. When The Man gave Rocco a .38 revolver to use if the game got out of hand he had no intention of using it. Now his insatiable appetite for money, that he used to shower others with gifts, had drawn the wrath of the underground.

Rocco was a marked man who didn't know whether he would live to see tomorrow's sunrise.

CHAPTER 6

Ben's Birthday Dinner

A parade of joggers beat out a mindless rhythm as it shuffled along the pathway in the park. Everyone in it took full command of their space, intimidating other pedestrians, oblivious to traffic lights or vehicular traffic.

The cool comfort of the morning soothed their bodies and embalmed the consciousness of their minds. They were suspended in a cognitive void, as they wove their way along the course, conscious of obstacles only when in danger of an imminent collision. At times like these a deft last minute move to the right or left usually avoided contact and required little conscious thought or effort. It was an exhilarating experience, lost in thought and heightened in intensity by the vivid colors around them – the aroma of a floral bouquet in the air and the chirping of birds announcing the arrival of a new day.

Bud and Ben joined the early morning ritual ambling along at half speed among the fleeting figures. The two men had built this routine into their daily schedule and followed it religiously – hangovers permitting. Usually both of them held the joggers in contempt since they considered walking to be much more civilized than aimless running. Often they were tempted to inadvertently stick out a foot as one of the bodies brushed by. It was a tempting thought but they left their needs wanting.

During these early morning journeys the two men addressed a wide range of issues in the course of their discussions. In addition to the stock market, business, politics, religion, current events, sports and details of their current holiday; time was sometimes found for more philosophical topics. Once they grappled with the meaning of life and another time the structure of the universe. Neither question, however, was solved. It was during discussions of more complex issues that their walks were prolonged in length.

On these longer walks they circumvented the Alai Wai Canal, Fort Derussey, the zoo and the topless beach located along the way to Diamond Head. It always took longer when the beach was included in the itinerary. At these times Tina and Janice became infuriated since their husbands returned later than usual. They knew Ben and Bud had been watching topless women flaunt their wares on the beach. However this wasn't the cause for annoyance; Tina wanted to hit the beach early since Pam and Alice always put in the morning shift while Janice expected Ben to take her out to breakfast every day.

* * * * * *

The Whites made sure they always had a cooking unit each year. Janice insisted on it. It had been three years, however, since she last cooked a meal in the condominium. That last meal was a memorable occasion which came very close to evolving into an eviction party. Tina was partly to blame.

It was Ben's birthday and both couples decided to have an informal dinner in one of their units. The Toppers agreed to bring dessert and the meat while the Whites provided the vegetables, salad and wine. Janice insisted on cooking in her unit since it boasted a brand new Jenne Aire stove. It didn't matter that none of them had ever used that kind of appliance before. After all as Janice had put it in response to Bud's incessant questioning:

"What the hell, a stove is a stove; any fool can turn one on. So piss off and don't bug me."

To show everyone just how adept she could be with the new stove Janice decided to also bake bread for the dinner to settle once and for all any question about her mastery of the new stove. She had never baked bread before in any oven but, in her opinion that didn't matter since any idiot could read a recipe.

While picking up steaks at the Food Pantry, Bud became convinced it would have been cheaper to eat out. However the Whites had made such a big deal out of cooking a gourmet dinner that anticipation for the meal overcame this concern and began to whet his appetite. He winced as the check-out register rang up the exorbitant bill.

"Christ, I'm not buying the store, just a few of the items in it," he announced to the smiling cashier as she pillaged through a small fortune in Bud's travelers checks. It was a good thing Tina hadn't come or it would have been even more expensive.

Bud's arms ached and his back protested intensely as he worked his way down the street on the trip back to the condo laden with groceries. The bags grew heavier each step of the way and he was forced to rest their weight on benches, newspaper dispensers and even the curb at various stages along the route home. Just as he began to entertain the thought of abandoning the groceries, fearing his arms would become permanently disabled, he finally arrived at the elevator in the building.

After a slow and painful trip the elevator finally stopped at Bud's floor. Now the trick was to get out of the elevator with all of his bags intact before the door closed shut. This was no easy task since he was by himself at this stage of the ascent. He began by dropping to his hands and knees and thrusting one leg against the elevator door while simultaneously edging each bag of groceries one at a time along the floor and out the door. The process worked well except that one bag remained out of reach. To get to it he had to leave his position of control in the door's pathway. A quick dart–first to the bag, then to the open button–would do it. He made it to the bag but looked in dismay as the door closed and the elevator proceeded up to the next floor.

Eventually Bud and all of his bags made it to the unit. Completely oblivious to his feat of such significant magnitude Tina demanded to know what took him so long.

Bud consoled himself with two screwdrivers while Tina challenged a bottle of red wine. It was getting close to time to leave for the White's when Tina decided to phone her sister in Seattle. After 20 minutes of gossip, and a mounting telephone bill, Bud began pacing the floor.

"Say goodbye! You're on long distance," he shouted to Tina.

She ignored him as the conversation continued. "What was that? I couldn't hear you with Bud ranting in the background. Shut up, Bud! I can't hear what Judy is saying."

"Say goodbye, goddamn it! This is costing a fortune!" It really got on his nerves when Tina stayed on long distance calls to talk about trivial things. He considered it the ultimate waste of money.

Tina wrinkled her nose and stuck out her tongue at Bud. "Well, I better go. Scrooge is shouting in the wings," she hissed into the telephone receiver. "See you when we get back."

Finally the Toppers were ready to go. Bud carried a paper bag laden with steaks and dessert while Tina brought a bottle of her favorite red wine. Even though the Whites had agreed to provide wine with dinner Tina wanted to make sure her brand was available.

As they approached the doorway to the White's apartment, shouting could be heard from inside the room.

"**Get off the bloody phone**!" Ben's voice screamed.

"See! It sounds like Janice is doing the same thing as you. Wasting money on long distance phone calls."

"Dry up!" Tina responded as she pounded on the door. A dead silence from inside the unit greeted the knock.

The door opened slowly and Ben's face suddenly appeared in the aperture. "Welcome, come into the Hawaiian telephone exchange," he invited. "Janice is doing her part to ensure that Bell is making money for its stockholders."

Janice was standing by her new stove with her back facing the guests. She was going through the motions of cooking – her figure intent on the pots strewn across the top of the stove.

"Alright everyone lighten up!" Tina commanded. "Telephones are an essential service, right Janice?"

"Right," came a rather subdued response. This was unlike Janice who usually was ready to party at all times.

"Hey Ben what's with Janice? Turn around Janice so we can yell at you," Bud quipped.

"You're too embarrassed to turn around aren't you?" Ben chimed in. "Ask Janice what happened to her this afternoon Tina. It was a hoot!"

"What happened Janice?" Tina asked.

"I was trying to be nice to the little kid in the unit next door and was playing with his goddamn toy," she replied, her back still facing everyone. "It was one of those suction toys which stick on the wall. Guess what happened?"

"What happened?" chorused Tina and Bud.

By this time Ben started laughing. He laughed until his face became beet red and tears started to well up in his eyes.

"This!!!" Janice announced as she whirled around to face the group.

Everyone, including Janice, roared with laughter. Dead center on her forehead was the biggest hickey they'd ever seen. While playing with the toy she had stuck it on her forehead announcing to the child that she was now a rhinoceros and should be treated with great respect. However when she tried to remove it, the toy remained stuck to her forehead. After several attempts the suction caused a plopping noise as she finally wrestled it from her forehead. A large, brown circular tattoo was left as a mark.

The hickey became a conversation piece as the dinner party progressed. More mundane events such as long distance telephone calls and Ben's sunburn were forgotten as the booze and conversation flowed.

"Hey Tina what is smooth, white and brown in the middle?" asked Bud.

"Christ it sounds like one of your dirty jokes," she replied. "I don't know and I couldn't care less."

"Give up? You give up?" Bud cried triumphantly. "It's Janice's forehead." He laughed uproariously, pleased with his wit. It didn't matter that everyone ignored him; he thought it was a good one.

The mouth watering aroma of baking bread wafted its way through the unit as the merriment progressed. It tempted Bud's nostrils as he became conscious of the smell.

"Hey Janice, that bread smells great. It looks like Ben is going to lose his bet. Did you know he bet me that you couldn't bake bread in your new oven? He actually offered odds, down at the Melting Pot."

"That goes to show how dumb he is. As soon as the bread comes out Tina and I are going to use the grill to cook steaks – better than you'll get in any restaurant. Right Tina?" Janice sounded pleased with herself as she gently rubbed the bruise on her forehead.

"You're damn right!" Tina shot back.

Shortly afterward it was time to remove the bread from the oven. Everyone peered over her shoulder as Janice proudly lifted the loaves from the oven.

"My God, they're little buggars," Ben observed as Janice carried the pans over to the countertop. "But they do smell great."

Bud also thought they seemed small. In fact they only filled each pan one-third full. He agreed with Ben, however, that the bread smelled damn good. His mouth watered at the thought of a slice of homemade bread as soon as it could be removed from the pans.

"You skeptics don't deserve any," Tina told the men. Just because it's a fancy new stove and because Janice has never baked bread before, you guys were making bets with the Admiral and some of the other reprobates down at the pub. Shame on you!"

Now it was time for the triumphant cutting of the bread. However Janice found it a bit difficult to cut with the knife. *Perhaps,* she thought, *it's because it's dull. Damn Ben! I told him to sharpen this knife.* With some difficulty she managed to cut one of the loaves into slices which were then served to her company.

"What is this a rock?" Ben shouted as his teeth bounced off the rigid object. His slice of bread was as tough as nails and weighed a ton.

The Toppers politely declined comment as Janice appeared close to tears.

"I don't understand what happened," she announced. "I followed the recipe exactly and put it in the oven when the dough was good and fresh."

"Didn't you leave the dough overnight to rise?" Tina asked.

"No. I didn't know it was supposed to rise overnight," she replied as she collected the remnants and was about to throw them in the garbage.

"Why don't you put it out for that stray dog who is always scrounging around for food," Ben suggested. "Here give it to me and I'll put it out in the entrance way. Let's get on with the rest of dinner."

The dog was lying in his usual place on the White's doorstep, waiting for treats they frequently offered him. He immediately pounced on the bread, sniffed it, turned up his nose, and sauntered over to the next doorstep. The bread sat there in solitude even a starving dog would have nothing to do with it.

"Tina have you ever used the grill on a Jenne Aire range before? I'm not sure how to work it," Janice asked, showing less confidence than before.

"What the hell, a grill is a grill. We'll throw on some vegetable oil so the steaks won't stick and then get on with it."

Both women busied themselves around the stove as Ben and Bud anticipated a delicious steak dinner. There were no bread or buns but there would be lots of salad and wine.

Suddenly smoke from the grill grew in intensity as the women proceeded to cook the steak. It wasn't long before thick black smoke impregnated the rest of the suite.

"What in hell is going on?" Ben bellowed. "Is this an indoor barbecue or what?"

By this time the smoke was unbearable. All of a sudden an ear-piercing scream echoed through the apartment; the smoke alarm had erupted in annoyance.

"How do you shut this goddamn thing off? The noise is shattering my eardrums!"

Soon a siren added its shrill scream to the cacophony of sound. It wasn't long before the firemen were at the door followed by the manager. A crowd of onlookers peered curiously at the scene; and the long awaited dinner became a disaster. Seeing it was a false alarm the firemen shrugged their shoulders and returned to their truck.

"**What the hell is going on**?" the manager demanded of the couples. "**Don't you even know how to operate a stove? What a bunch of stupid hicks.**"

Tina had planned to stay out of the melee but the last insult was more than she was prepared to take. "**Who in hell are you calling a hick you sawed off little bastard?**" she demanded of the manager. "**Bud, punch this little creep out before I get mad.**"

Janice and Ben moved from one adversary to the other trying to calm things down since they were tenants in the apartment. However once Tina got her dander up she wasn't easily dissuaded.

"**Get the hell out of here!**" she shouted at the manager as the little man beat a hasty retreat. His tiny legs pumped like pistons as he dashed down the hallway trying to escape Tina's wrath.

"**And take this with you!**" she screamed, as a loaf of Janice's bread followed him down the hallway. It careened off the wall just behind his head, broke a hallway light fixture and dented the door of one of the other apartments.

"Well Janice at least we found a use for your bread," Tina shouted triumphantly as the little man disappeared from sight. "Now let's have a drink."

The two couples were sipping their drinks, trying to salvage something from the shambles of Ben's birthday party, when the phone rang.

Ben jumped up to get it. "Hello, hello, is anybody on the line?"

"B-b-ben, is that you?" responded a muffled voice. "B-b-ben, I'm in trouble and need your help."

"Who is this? What's the problem?" Ben responded.

Click!!!

The phone went dead.

"Ben, who was that on the phone?"

"I think it was Rocco."

CHAPTER 7

The Soul Singer

"Hot damn that was a hell of a dinner," burped Ben as the four vacationers ambled out of the Mexican restaurant. They had stumbled onto the new eating place while going on an evening stroll. It was a new discovery that called for a return visit.

"I would have enjoyed it more if Bud hadn't tricked me into eating the green dip," Janice replied tersely. Her tongue still smarted from the hot salsa she had eaten.

Prior to beginning the meal Janice had consumed huge quantities of taco chips embellished with red salsa. Noticing her rate of consumption Bud suggested she try the green dip which, he assured her, was mild. Instead of gingerly sampling the concoction, Janice took Bud at his word and loaded a chip with the newly recommended sauce. She devoured it all at once. Her act was immediately followed by an eruption which brought the restaurant to a dead stop.

"Jeeeeeesssuuusss!! What the hell have you done to me? Bud you poisoned me you bastard!" Janice screamed while lashing out for the water jug and upsetting the table and its contents in the process.

"Hey Janice you can cool it by whistling," Bud taunted.

Bud's smartass response drew a reaction from Tina. Now he was in for it. During the melee Ben said and did nothing. There was no point sharing in the hostility which the two women directed at Bud.

Shortly afterward calm prevailed, followed by a strained silence. However as the meal continued the tempo picked up, the incident forgotten. As the second liter of wine grew into the third, the party became louder and more flippant. It was about this time that Tina and Janice noticed how young the waiter was. He was still in his teens with an air of innocence that amused the women. When asked, he said it was his first job as a waiter. After washing dishes at the restaurant for several weeks he had talked the manager into giving him a chance to wait table, replacing one of the waiters who failed to show up for a shift. He was out to make a good impression at all costs.

"Hey honey what's your name? You're doing a good job for someone so young," Tina cooed.

"Jack," came the response.

"Well Jack I'll bet all the girls at school would like to crawl into your pants," she teased.

In spite of the red blush which crept across his face Jack smiled at the comment in a good natured way. As the evening wore on his visits to the table became more frequent and longer in duration. It was obvious the diners and the waiter enjoyed each others' company. If it wasn't for the frequent disapproving glances of the head waiter the camaraderie would have been great. Eventually the Whites and Toppers finished dinner and prepared to leave.

"Listen Jack we really appreciate the service you gave us this evening, especially since it's your first night on the job. This is for you, put it in your jeans and don't share it," Tina offered.

"But we're supposed to share our tips with the others."

"No way. This is for you only."

The party stumbled out of the restaurant and began its journey back to the condos. This had been their first visit to the restaurant and they looked forward to returning.

The next night the couples returned to the bistro and were greeted by a different waiter.

"Where's Jack? We want Jack to serve us," Janice demanded.

"Oh he got canned. Apparently he was flirting with two old broads last night and he also tried to hold back on a tip. Can you imagine, his first night on the job and he screwed up like that."

"Let's get the hell out of here," Tina cried.

Dinner that night was much more subdued than during the previous evening as they ate in one of the neighboring restaurants. Conversation was reserved and after consuming a liter of wine the party was ready to leave. Bud and Ben were anxious to head straight back to the condos for a nightcap and an early evening. They had big plans for the following morning. The nude beach was scheduled for their morning walk and that was a requisite for an early start. As they made their way up Kalakaua Avenue the loud beat of Motown music saturated the air.

"**I heard it through the grapevine.**" The reverberation stopped Tina dead in her tracks.

"Listen Janice he's great. Sounds just like Marvin Gaye."

"Who's that, one of the California raisins?" Bud queried. Both he and Ben were into country music.

"We've got to go in," the women chimed as they quickly made their way toward the noise. They rushed into the doorway of a small club and peered at the singer on stage.

"**Hi there young ladies, cum'on in,**" the singer invited as he paused between songs. "**And bring those old men with you,**" he quipped as Ben and Bud appeared in the doorway.

As they made their way to the only vacant table in the club the singer began his version of *Under the Boardwalk*. It was exciting as the sounds of the 60s and 70s were reproduced live, and even better than the originals.

"My God he's good," Tina proclaimed. "I'm not leaving here til closing time."

That announcement shot Ben and Bud's early morning plans all to hell. However they didn't mind since their taste in music extended to stuff from the 60s and 70s.

"Where y' all from?" asked the voice from the stage. "And what'd y' all like to hear?"

"Seattle," Ben shot back, "and we like country." He was pleased with his quick response since he thought it unlikely a rock singer could launch into a medley of country songs.

In response the singer launched into the *Yodeling Song*. It was an upbeat number that caught the audience's attention and drew them in as the singer worked all of them into the text of the song. The yodeling became faster and faster. His versatility and talent enthralled the audience and they clapped to the beat.

The room was electric as the clapping gained in frenzy in an attempt to keep up with the excitement on stage. It wasn't long before Janice found a way to work her shrill whistling into the fray.

"Tweeet! ... Tweeeeeeet! ... Tweeeeeeeeeeeeet!"

Janice whistled faster and louder as the beat went on, increasing in intensity until the audience's eardrums cried out in protest. Finally, with hands smarting and ears ringing, the audience expressed its appreciation as the song ended. A standing ovation greeted the band at this point.

"All right now let's get on down," the singer shouted as he grinned from ear to ear.

The audience greeted this announcement with cheers and began chanting and jumping up and down. Ben, however, promptly sat down; he intended to comply with the request literally.

At the end of the set the singer moved from table to table, greeting each member of the audience personally. He quipped with them and shot back the proffered B-29 at each table before moving on to the next. He was a picture of contrast as he made his way around the darkened room. His snow white suit and pearly teeth contrasted sharply with his black ebony skin. Eventually the entertainer arrived at the table of the Seattle crew.

"Hi, y'all. Mind if I sit down? My name is Rick. I'm planning to buy a condo – maybe you can help me."

* * * * *

Rick's Early Years

Rick was raised in a small fishing village by the name of Sherno, located 30 miles south of Stewart, Alaska. He and his family were the only blacks in a community of whites and Native Indians. He was the offspring of two seasonal shore workers.

Life in the village was dull and routine. The villagers put in long hard hours during the short salmon season during the summer followed by frequent periods of inactivity during the subsequent winter. Fishing was the only means of livelihood in the small community of 1500. During each short salmon season the village was a frenzy of activity; with the annual arrival of the slippery, silver hoard of fish came an influx of boats and fishermen from as far down the coast as San Diego. At this time of year the coastline of Alaska became a wild frontier inundated with a mass of humanity searching for the silver treasure. They arrived at the dock travelling on anything that could float. It was a fierce competition in which only the fittest were winners. In addition to dedicated fishermen who had elected that type of work as a way of life, it also drew hardworking people from other vocations, and a motley crew of opportunists from all walks of life. Some were college students on a summer job or loggers who changed their line of work at this time of year. Others were winos, card sharks and con men out to make a quick buck. Saturday nights belonged to the fishermen. They converged on Sherno with a vengeance, bent on drinking, gambling and fighting.

Since the fishing grounds were closed on weekends, dozens of boats were tied side by side and end to end adjacent to the docks and overflowing into most of the harbor. As the drinking began each night, grudges initiated on the fishing grounds the previous week often erupted into brawls. This was their night to party as the next day would bring with it the inevitable hangovers and a return to the grounds for another week of fishing. An air of danger and excitement always accompanied the arrival of the boats.

Rick loved it!

As a small boy he had looked forward, with anticipation, to the arrival of summer and the corresponding return of the boats. He hated the long dismal winters in which nothing of interest happened. In the summer he even tolerated the rancid stench of the fish reduction plant since it coincided with the return of the boats.

The reduction plant processed waste products generated from the fish cannery. Fish heads and innards were rendered into fertilizer and cooking oil. It only operated at certain times during the week when sufficient waste from the cannery warranted a run. At these times an acrid stink permeated the air. It oozed into every nook and cranny, saturating clothes and penetrating the pores of each resident in the village. The smell resembled that of burning, rotten fish. Needless to say it was not one of the most popular areas in which to work.

During the season some boats unloaded their catch directly at the cannery while others delivered to fish packers on the grounds. The fish packers, in turn, delivered their fish to the Talley dock at the cannery. On the Talley dock workmen called "fish pitchers" unloaded boats by pitching fish from the holds onto the dock for sorting. To pitch fish they used a tool called a fish pew, consisting of a long wooden handle, to which was attached a curved metal spike at one end. It resembled a pitch fork used for hay, with only one blade. The "fish pitcher" would pierce the head of the salmon with the spike and throw it out of the hold. Once the fish landed on the dock a different shore worker, called a tallyman, separated them into one of the five salmon species and sent one type at a time into the cannery along another conveyer belt for weighing and forwarding to separate bins for further processing. The tallyman had to be quick to recognize each type of salmon and often caught only a glimpse of part of the fish's body before it went up the conveyer belt.

Rick's favorite hangout during the week was the Talley dock. He never tired of watching the handling of fish and soon became as adept as a tallyman at identifying one species of salmon from another. This was no small feat for a ten-year-old boy since many of the grown men who were "fish pitchers" could not tell the subtle differences among the types of fish.

At this time in his young life Rick's ambition was to be a fisherman and join the fleet when it went to the grounds each Sunday. But he would settle in the meantime for an opportunity to work on the Talley dock – if they would only give him a chance. As long as he stayed out of their way the men working on the dock tolerated him. On occasion, however, he got underfoot and had to make a quick departure, accompanied by a flow of curses. This arrangement could have continued successfully for the rest of the summer if not for two events which occurred in close succession. The first dealt with his attempt to wash down the Talley dock and the second with his recently acquired interest in becoming a drummer in a band.

In an attempt to become useful on the Talley dock Rick had picked up a hose and was washing down a section of the dock after some fish had been removed from it. Normally he was not allowed into the work area since it was dangerous for a child and he was likely to get in the way. But in this instance the tallyman was busy with one of the seine boat skippers who had just delivered a load of salmon and the fish pitchers were busy tying up a packer which had just arrived for unloading. It was Rick's big chance. He could show the men how helpful he was and perhaps earn their respect as a fellow worker.

The hose was open to full force as Rick continued with his task. It was all he could do to hold onto it because of the tremendous pressure of the water. He was about half finished when one of the fish pitchers noticed him and shouted for the boy to get out of there. As Rick turned in the direction of the sound the nozzle of the hose turned with him. He dropped the hose and ran for his life as the cursing tallyman, arms flailing wildly, fell overboard under the force of the water from the hose. Rick didn't return to the Talley dock for the rest of the week. He knew his presence would not be well received. However several days later he took up his usual position, overseeing the fish as they moved up the conveyor belt and past the busy tallyman. He made sure that he was situated far enough out of reach to ensure a safe retreat if necessary.

As the fish continued on their journey into the cannery Rick began a rhythmic and incessant beat on the side of the conveyer belt, using a fish pew which had been discarded by one of the shore workers. His drumming got louder and louder as he was caught up in the beat.

Rap! ... Rap! ... Rap! ...

Rick found the constant beat hypnotic as he settled into his favorite activity.

* * * * *

Ever since he had taken up the drums Rick had drummed on everything; furniture, dishes, cars, steps, and sidewalks. Even dogs and cats were the unwilling recipients of the tapping of his drumsticks. He drove his teacher, parents and friends mad with his incessant beating on every object within reach. His interest in drumming began with records of Philip Sousa in the music appreciation class at school, but gained significantly in contrast and momentum with *Jailhouse Rock* by Elvis Presley and *Wipe-out* by the Ventures.

In an attempt to interest him in another musical instrument Rick's mother purchased a guitar for his tenth birthday. Instead of launching into chords on the guitar, as a welcome respite from his drumming, Rick proceeded to beat the instrument with his drum sticks. He was nurturing a habit which grated on everyone's nerves.

* * * * *

Rick was totally engrossed with his drumming on the conveyer belt. Closing his eyes he became Gene Krupa. In the daydream his beat became the rage of the nation as audiences cheered his every move. Television interviewers competed for his attention and beautiful women vied for his notice. He was enjoying his escape into a fantasy world as the beat went on when suddenly he was jarred back into reality!

"I've got yuh, ya little bastard! See how ya like a trip inta the drink!"

Rick's body cut a cervical swath as it soared into the air, over the log pilings on the edge of the dock, and into the murky salt water adjacent to them. He spluttered and coughed as his head broke surface, to the laughter of all the men on the Talley dock.

"That'll teach ya sonny, only men're allowed down here!" shouted the tallyman.

Rick retreated home humiliated beyond belief. His shoes squished as he walked and his shirt and pants clung to his body – every move felt restricted and awkward. He was too embarrassed to return to the dock the following day. Instead he brooded at home longing for a way to save face and to force the men to accept him as an equal. The next Saturday night provided that opportunity.

It promised to be a particularly boisterous evening, following a very successful week on the fishing grounds. A huge run of salmon had appeared that week and seine boats brailed their silver treasure aboard after almost every set. The holds of the packers were filled to the top and the cannery was running at full capacity. When Saturday arrived the fishers were eager to celebrate the big week. It was still early in the evening when the local jail was filled to the brim with intoxicated fishermen. The local sheriff who routinely appointed a dozen deputies each weekend to help keep the peace was pressed to find another place to detain the growing number of clients. To meet this need he decided to use one of the retorts in the cannery as a jail.

A retort is a large cylindrical oven in which cases of canned salmon are cooked. It is large enough for a grown man to stand up in and it could hold up to twenty prisoners at a time. The sheriff thought it was an ideal container since the huge iron cover on both ends could only be opened or closed from the outside. After the men sobered up the next morning his plan was to fine them and then send them back to their homes or boats.

Rick peered through the darkness of the idle cannery as the deputies arrived periodically to throw more men into the retort. It was pitch black in the oven and the front end was left open only enough to provide air for the inhabitants. As their work progressed, the deputies were not aware that each time they deposited a fisherman in the front end of the retort; Rick opened the back end and allowed him to escape. Near the end of the evening the sheriff and his deputies thought the retort was full and did not make any more arrests. The next morning, when they went to let the men out they were astounded to find no one there. It wasn't long before Rick's exploit made the rounds of the fishermen and shore workers. He had salvaged his young reputation on the docks and was once again tolerated by the men.

For the rest of the season Rick was allowed to return to his vantage point near the Talley dock and to even help out now and then when it got busy. As summer grew into fall Rick dreaded the return of another dreary winter. School held little interest for him and he desperately sought an avenue of escape.

He found it in the world of music.

His interest in drumming, which he had originally nurtured for the sole purpose of annoying people, now broadened to include singing and playing the guitar. As new pop songs made the charts Rick memorized the words and sang with the artist each time it was played. Not only did he sing the same words but he also imitated the voice. His renditions of *Blueberry Hill* by Satchmo and *Walking to New Orleans* by Fats Domino were very good imitations, enjoyed by all of his classmates. He had a natural flair for singing and this talent made him popular at school. It wasn't long before Rick formed a band, called the ***Bock Gees***, with two of his buddies.

When Rick's sixteenth birthday arrived he had great expectations. He was now old enough to drive a car, to get a job the following summer in the fishing industry and, hopefully, to convince a girl to help him lose his virginity. He had been more than willing to lose the latter attribute ever since his thirteenth birthday but the right opportunity never arose. He had engaged in heavy necking and petting on numerous occasions but couldn't quite make the final plunge. His growing popularity as a vocalist and leader of a rock and roll band should've enhanced the likelihood of that event.

* * * * *

As summer approached once again he spent more and more time during classes shut off in his own dream world, fantasizing about two major undertakings.

The first involved the coming summer. He wanted to ship out on a seine boat so badly he could almost taste it. In his ongoing daydream he was the hero who saved a gigantic catch of salmon for the boat. In this fantasy he arrived in port with a deck load of silvers where he impressed the girls with thousands of dollars stuffed in his pockets.

In the second fantasy Rick dreamed of his English teacher, Miss Renton. She had beautifully curved legs that seemed to go on forever. Her heavy breasts strained against the tight sweaters she often wore and caused Rick to lose track of whatever else he was supposed to be thinking about. In his daydreams he spent many hours caressing her nipples and pressing his thighs against hers. These adolescent daydreams consumed all of his creative thought, at the expense of his schoolwork.

Summer arrived at last but he couldn't land a job on a boat. No one wanted an inexperienced kid on the crew. Luckily he was eventually hired to pitch fish on his beloved Talley dock. It was his second choice but still a dream come true. Imagine a sixteen-year-old who knew fish as well as an experienced tallyman. He was anxious to prove himself right from the first day. It wasn't long, however, before the glamour wore off. Standing up to his ass in fish scales and slime was not his idea of fun. Within two weeks he quit that job and looked more favorably at another one in the office. It wasn't romantic but at least it was warm and dry.

Rick, however, still wanted to get on a boat. He pestered the skippers whenever they appeared in the office for cash advances or for advice from the manager on which area to fish the following week.

Finally, he hit pay dirt!

The crew from one of the boats had walked off and the skipper was desperate for an entire new team. He was prepared to take Rick as a skiff man the following Sunday.

Rick was ecstatic!

Imagine a sixteen-year-old going out on a fish boat for adventure as a full fledged skiff man. He had no idea what the position involved, but was sure it was a job of great prestige and importance.

To celebrate his new position Rick purchased an expensive set of rubber gear – bright yellow in color. It included a sou'wester cap, a pair of bib overalls, a top jacket and a pair of enormous rubber boots with deep treads on the soles. Rick thought he looked dashing in his new outfit as he paraded through the cannery and on the streets of the village.

It didn't matter that the sun was shining and it was very warm that day and causing him to sweat profusely inside the outfit, he was announcing to the world that he had come of age. He was a full fledged fisherman destined for adventure and glory on the high seas. It was particularly important to him to impress the girls in his class, especially Amanda, the blonde girl with the tight ass and sexy legs.

A cadre of girls promised to see him off the next Sunday afternoon. They gathered at the dock, giggling and waving to Rick, as the boat prepared to leave. Rick scurried around untying lines and coiling them on the boat's deck. It was a proud day for him as he realized his big dream. By the end of the week he would return, victorious from his battle with the sea and with big bucks in his pockets.

As the boat headed out of the harbor Rick postured for the audience on the dock – standing upright at the bow, one hand shielding his eyes as his profile looked toward the horizon. He thought he cut an impressive figure – clothed in his bright yellow rubber gear. He was sure his fans on shore could still see him and it was important to leave a lasting impression. In his mind he fancied himself a swashbuckling adventurer out to conquer the world.

Five days later the boat returned. A large group of onlookers were on the dock to greet it. Among them the same giggly girls who had arrived to pay homage to their fisherman hero, Rick. After the tie up was completed Rick was still nowhere in sight. The girls were disappointed since they had looked forward to his triumphant return – a man home from a dangerous journey.

Suddenly a figure clad in yellow appeared in the doorway of the ship's galley – its face a ghostly white as it staggered across the deck. When the figure attempted to vault over the side of the boat and onto the dock it fell head first into the water.

The hero's triumphant return had been seriously compromised. Rick had been seasick from the moment the boat left the harbor the previous Sunday. His short career in fishing came to an abrupt end!

Fishing is for animals! Rick thought as he posted a notice on the bulletin board, advertising a brand new set of rubber gear for sale. He was happy to return to the boring confines of the company office. The next two years passed quickly. His band had now become well known and was in demand in Stewart as well as Sherno. Groupies followed them around. Sex was fast and easy and Rick made sure he had his share.

In spite of the availability of many girls he lusted after a beautiful red head five years his senior. Rick had first noticed her at the checkout counter in the supermarket. He had followed her voluptuous figure as she pushed a grocery cart up and down the aisles. Her long legs and flat thighs were poured into a short, tight, leather mini dress. Rotund shapes protruded like melons from under her blouse, hinting of the delights contained under it.

This called for strategic planning. It was important that when she was in produce, Rick inspect the lettuce in case his mother may want to buy some later; when she was at the meat counter, he was there to check out the prices; and when she was in canned goods, Rick thought he should be there in case she needed help to reach something on the top shelf. When she arrived at the check out counter Rick was right behind her. She had a full shopping cart. Rick had a pack of gum.

The redhead fumbled for money in her purse to pay the cashier and accidently dropped a dollar bill onto the floor. Rick was about to pick it up when he thought better of it. If he waited for her to bend down to pick it up he would get a much better look at the wondrous shapes protruding from her partially opened blouse. As he stared directly at her chest she smiled at him coyly.

"Can I help you carry your groceries?" Rick heard himself say.

"That would be nice," she replied.

When they arrived at her apartment he followed the young lady in. It was several hours before he left wearing a smile on his face that went on forever.

Her name was Ella. She had arrived recently from San Diego to join her husband who was a fisherman. He had decided to move to Alaska in pursuit of halibut, a bottom fish, plentiful in the Bering Sea. They had been in Sherno now for three months and she hated every minute of it. She was left home frequently with nothing to do while he plied the sea as a crewman on one of the local halibut boats. Ella found life in Sherno dreadfully boring and was always on the lookout for excitement – today Rick was it.

Ella's husband was a wild, rangy tang character by the name of Thug who was old enough to be her father. Thug came by his name honestly since he was often in bar room brawls where he was feared for his ruthlessness with a knife. In fact he had done time in prison once for cutting a man's ear off in a fight several years earlier.

He was a big man – tall with a large frame. On one occasion he got into an altercation with the entire crew of one of the large seiners. After slugging two of the men and knocking them both unconscious, Thug pulled a knife from his boot and went after the other crew members. They began to run down the boardwalk trying to flee from this crazy man – Thug in full pursuit.

"**Back to the boats you bastards. Back to the boats!**" Thug thundered as he chased them down the walkway.

Thug was always on the make. When he put his mind to it he could charm the pants off the ladies. He could spin yarns about his escapades, both real and imagined. His tales always gained an attentive audience – both male and female. This trait contrasted with his violent temper which caused other men to avoid getting into arguments with him.

Although he was a fisherman by trade Thug had a weak stomach. In rough weather he was usually found in the foc'sle lying on his bunk. Seasick beyond belief. He wasn't available for wheel watch or for deck work when the boat began bucking the sea. Although others had to fill in for him, no one dared chastise him for it otherwise they would fall victim to his fists after arrival back on shore.

One evening shortly after the encounter in the supermarket, Rick was in bed enjoying the pleasures of the redheaded temptress when Thug returned home unexpectedly. A storm had driven the halibut boat back to port and the fishing trip had been postponed.

Thug suddenly appeared in the doorway of the bedroom. Rick stiffened in fear as a knife flashed in the darkness. He reacted instantly, jumping through the window and into the street.

He was naked except for his socks.

Rick had six blocks to travel home in sub-zero weather without a stitch on. The streak was on as he churned through the streets at top speed.

God it was cold!

"Hey, Rick! Is that all of you that's flying in the breeze?"

It was the giggling voice of Amanda, the girl he liked at school. **How embarrassing!**

It was time to get out of Sherno before Thug caught him on the street.

Rick arrived in Stewart shortly afterward and arranged to work his way by freight boat to San Francisco. He spent several years in the city by the sea, entertaining in bars and picking up odd jobs whenever possible. He had no plans to return to Sherno as long as Thug still walked the streets.

As Rick perfected his act he began to draw a following of loyal fans. Eventually he decided to ply his trade in Hawaii and had been there now for fifteen years.

CHAPTER 8

A New Discovery
At The Beach

The muffled sound of the phone rang in the distance. It was barely audible as the Whites fumbled with the lock on their apartment door. Janice, always infatuated with telephones, was anxious to reach it before it stopped.

"Get the lead out! We're going to miss it if you keep playing with that bloody lock."

"Piss off!" Ben hissed as he flung the door open.

Janice lunged through the doorway and tackled the phone in an attempt to salvage the call.

"Hello! Hello! Anybody there?"

A hollow, raspy voice whispered back; its eerie quality sent a chill down her spine. The voice was familiar but had a ghostly quality to it. Her face paled and the blood drained from her lips as she handed the receiver to Ben.

"Who the hell is it?"

"I'm not sure, but it sounds like Rocco. His voice is weird, almost as if he's calling from the grave." "Hello, Rocco. Is that you? This is Ben."

Dead silence!

"Rocco, are you there? Where are you? Are you all right?"

"B-b-ben, I'm in tr-r-r-ouble," the voice said.

"Where are you? Let me know where you are and I'll pick you up."

"I c-c-c-an't Ben. Gotta go."

Click!!!

The severed communication was abrupt and absolute. There was a finality to the sharp break in conversation, as if a prediction of no further contact in the future.

"Shit!"

"Why does he keep on calling and then hanging up before we can find out where the son-of-a-bitch is? I'm frustrated as hell!"

"Don't get uptight Ben. There is nothing you can do unless he phones back. Maybe deep down he doesn't really want to be helped."

The call threw a damper on the evening. After a shot of Scotch Ben resigned himself to a restless night.

It took forever for the next morning to arrive. After a fitful sleep Ben awoke exhausted.

"I have to meet Bud in fifteen minutes. Christ my eyes feel like sandpaper and I ache from head to toe. I feel the pits. How 'bout you?"

"M-m-m-m-ph." A muffled response came from under the covers. Janice had sunk completely under the sheet, her body straddled across the entire bed and a pillow was plunked on top of her head. She was completely oblivious to Ben's discomfort.

As Ben ranted and raved on about his misfortune Janice ignored him. She stretched out in comfort, savoring the warmth and serenity of the soft, comfortable bed. She didn't have much sympathy for Ben – if he was stupid enough to get up at this ungodly hour to go for a walk that was his business.

"Well, aren't you a conversation piece this morning!" he shouted. "I may as well be talking to the wall."

"M-m-m-mph."

Ben didn't wait for any further response as he slammed the door shut.

* * * * *

By this time the foursome's daily routine had expanded to include a night-time component. At Tina's insistence the itinerary now included a visit to Rick's show every night of the week except one – his night off. Each evening she insisted on what she called only a brief visit to the performance. Her idea of a brief visit, however, began with greetings at the start of the show and didn't end until the last set in the wee hours of the morning.

Ben and Bud had become exhausted. This schedule was fine for the women who slept in each morning but it played havoc with the early morning walks the men liked to engage in.

"Thank God this vacation is almost over," Bud announced one afternoon while at Pam and Alice's section of the beach. "I'm getting too tired to keep this bloody pace up. I need to go back to work for a rest."

"Aw quit yer bitchin'!" Pam roared out.

"Who's talkin' to you, ya fat old fart," Bud shot back.

In response Pam's eyes narrowed into slits and her nostrils flared. She glowered at Bud. Her breath came in quick gulps as she held it momentarily and then hissed it out through pursed lips. Her quick glance in Alice's direction brought the other woman into action – the team's second member circled behind Bud, crouching down like a tackle in a football game, ready to pounce. The rolls of fatty tissue bulged from her swimsuit, giving her the appearance of a huge sumo wrestler. Bud's eyes darted from one to the other. Panic began to show on his face.

"Okay, rip his shorts off! That'll fix the bastard!"

Sensing disaster Bud's reflexes instantly came into play. He quickly vaulted over a couple lying in the sand and scrambled up the bank to safety, where Ben was contentedly sunning himself in the shade.

"Christ those two old bags are crazy! Remember what they did to those tourists last year? No way was I going to defend my bathing suit against both of them."

"Macho move Bud. Two little old ladies scared the hell out of you."

"Who the hell are you to talk? You're not exactly mister dynamic yourself.

For the rest of the afternoon Bud kept a respectful distance from Pam and Alice. He made sure they were always within his peripheral vision just in case they made a move. Imagine if they ripped off his swimsuit on the crowded beach. He could visualize the ensuing write-up in the paper:

Man walks nude on Waikiki Beach! Two senior citizens shocked by exhibitionist – See page 8 for first hand account by Pam and Alice.

Bud decided to seek sanctuary on Terri and Mia's section of beach. It was far enough away from the old ladies to ensure sufficient warning if they decided to attack. Feeling relatively safe he stretched out on his beach mat and began to soak up the sun.

While relaxing in feline fashion Bud gazed into the distance where the birdlike silhouette of a plane, soaring upward into the azure blue sky, caught his attention. As he watched, the plane continued its ascent until it reached the appropriate altitude. At that point its line of flight leveled off to become horizontal with the ground and the plane proceeded into the distance and out of sight. Glancing to his right he could make out the outline of the majestic mountains of the Koolau range which framed the backdrop for the University of Hawaii. Returning his attention back to the departed plane he reflected on its implication for him.

God, he muttered, *in four days that'll be me on the way back home to the rain and cold. What a dismal thought.*

He quickly turned his attention to the sights on the beach around him. Figures were strewn in all directions on the sparkling white sand. They came in a variety of colors – the pallid white of new arrivals; the crimson red of those with an overdose of sun, done too quickly; and the various shades of brown glistening on bodies of the well-oiled regulars. Added to these sights were the smells of the day – the tangy, salty sea air titillated his nostrils intermingling with the various odors of lotion emanating from baking bodies.

In the sand on his immediate left lay the glistening body of a bronze Amazon – sun-bleached blonde hair contrasting with golden brown skin. Her taut calves, tantalizing thighs and the sensuous curve of her back were in total submission to the sun's pleasure. Her companion was a lobster of a man, growing redder as each hour passed. This evening would bring about the heat and pain of a severe sunburn – a test of the pleasure of a tropical holiday.

Out of the corner of his eye he noticed the arrival of a couple who were familiar fixtures at the seaside at this time of day. They visited Hawaii at the same time each year but seldom acknowledged or spoke to others at the beach. He watched them find a spot, smooth out the sand and roll out their beach mats.

After completing this ritual the male stood lookout over the rest of the beach posturing for his imagined fans. His well-muscled body hinted of regular workouts at a gym and earned him the nickname 'Charles Atlas.' His blonde wife always brought expensive jewelry to the beach and wore only custom designed bikinis. The few times she did acknowledge others was to announce loudly they only stayed in a penthouse when they came to Waikiki and to drop names of celebrities they had met. His nickname and her blondness, combined with their posh habits, earned them nicknames among the regulars such as 'Charles and Lady Di.'

"Christ," Bud uttered aloud. "He's posing again."

Looking more closely Bud noticed they had both developed paunches since the previous year. In fact they had made substantial weight gains.

"Hey Ben!" he shouted. "Charles and Lady Di do everything together. Now they're both pregnant."

Ben took no notice of the comment since he was busy plotting the coordinates of the blond Amazon Bud had ogled earlier. She had now turned over on her back with her untied bikini top forgotten in the sand. Her snow white breasts, sharply contrasting with her dark brown body, gave the appearance of two ice-cream cones, embellished with pink cherries on the top.

A sudden commotion caught the attention of the beachgoers. Yelling and shouting came from close by and a uniformed policeman appeared from among the crowd.

"You dirty old man! I warned you not to have anything to do with my niece!" an emotional voice screamed over the din. It was Terri.

"That's him officer, that's the man! I want to lay a charge!"

"What's the problem lady?"

"That dirty old man was molesting my niece. He's always after young women and he drinks all the time over at that pub. You should also close that pub down."

"Hold on lady. One thing at a time. Okay buddy what've you got to say?"

"She's crazy. Me and my girlfriend were just holding hands and this old broad attacked us."

"I know you! I know you! You're a disgrace for an old age pensioner! You dirty old man!"

"Piss off lady! Mind your own business. Why don't you ask your niece?"

By this time Bud recognized the gravelly quality of the old man's voice. It was the Admiral.

"How about it young lady? Is this man bothering you?" the officer asked.

"I'm so embarrassed. No, he is a friend of mine. Auntie why don't you mind your own business?"

"He pinched your bum! I saw him officer. I'm laying a charge. Take this down. My name is Terri Gowans. That's Terri, spelt with an i."

"What's your age young lady? Do you support this charge?"

"I'm twenty-eight and this is ridiculous. Come on Addie baby. Let's go to the pub for a drink."

The policeman shrugged his shoulders at this point and walked away, followed by the Admiral and his young girlfriend. The couple beat a hasty retreat to the safety of the Melting Pot.

"What's going on Bud?" Tina and Janice had returned from the other section of the beach where they had been visiting the crotchety old women.

"Oh I think Terri and the Admiral have something going. She caught him with another woman and she went into a jealous fit."

"That true Terri?"

"I won't honor Bud's stupid remark with a comment," she replied.

"Cum'on Bud, we're going shopping with Janice and Ben."

"I'm not!"

Bud hated to shop – Tina lived for it.

"Come on Bud I've got a car," Ben added. "We're only going to pick up groceries. Be back in an hour and you can catch the sun again before it goes down."

"I don't know. I hate to miss my beach time."

"Quit sniveling Bud. We need more groceries so let's go," Tina demanded.

"Okay as long as it's only for an hour."

It proved to be Bud's longest hour!

* * * * *

They had no sooner started out on the ride when Ben took the wrong turn onto a one way street. Traffic swarmed angrily around them whizzing by on either side – horns honking and fists shaking out of windows.

"Ben you idiot! You can't navigate your way around the block!" Janice screamed.

"Can too. Watch my wash."

A break in traffic provided the opportunity. With tires squealing and black smoke trailing behind, the car reversed its direction and broke into the rhythm of the traffic flow.

"Ben d'you know the way to the Holiday Food Mart? That's where we're supposed to be going you know."

"Sure Janice. Piece of cake."

The car darted in and out of the traffic as it proceeded on its journey, supposedly travelling in the direction of the Food Mart. However when Filthy McNasty's pawn shop appeared on the right side of the car for the third time Bud began to doubt Ben's command of direction.

A voice shot out from the back seat. "Ben you should have turned left at the last light!"

"Don't worry – be happy. I'm just following this bus in front of us."

"Yeah! Well why are there no other cars on this street?"

"How the hell should I know? Ask the bus driver." By this time even Ben was becoming exasperated.

"But the sign over there says 'Buses Only'. What's that blue flashing light behind us?"

"Hell it's the cops," Ben responded. "Watch my wash!"

A quick turn of the wheel and a slam of the brakes produced a one hundred and eighty degree change in direction. Now they were not only driving in a buses only lane but they were also travelling in the wrong direction on a one way street. The cop car, with lights flashing, sat astride the street calmly awaiting Ben's arrival.

Ben screeched to a stop in front of the police cruiser. The man in blue strode over to the window as Ben rolled it down.

"Yes officer is something wrong?" Ben's voice was one of innocence and respect.

"Somethin' wrong? Hell there ain't nothin' yer doin' that's right. Let's have a look at yer drivers license Mac."

"One moment Officer. I need to consult with my legal counsel who also happens to be navigator of this car. Bud this is Officer ... what did you say your name was? He wants to see my driver's license. Should we show it to him?"

"Christ! Just show it to him so we can get the hell out of here. I never should've let you guys talk me into this stupid shopping trip."

"Awright Buddy," the policeman demanded, "Let's see yer license or I'm bookin' ya and maybe yer navigator too!"

"Show it to him dummy!" Janice snapped.

"Alright officer here it is. My only crime was to be misled by a bus. I trusted it and look what happened."

"Smart ass ain't ya! I'm writing ya up for goin' the wrong way on a one way street and fer operation of a motor vehicle in a restricted zone. Yer lucky I'm such a nice guy or you'd be on yer way to the station fer not cooperating."

After the altercation the expedition proceeded to the Ala Moana Shopping Center – the Holiday Food Mart forgotten.

The women excitedly planned their attack on the shopping center while the men seethed. Ben was annoyed about the traffic tickets he had just received while Bud, regretfully watching the sun fade into the afternoon, saw his beach time disappear.

* * * * *

The afternoon had quickly turned to early evening which brought with it the routine visit to the pub.

Bud was checking on the Pu Pus when the Admiral walked in with a new young broad. She wore a skin tight miniskirt and black lace pantyhose with several holes in each leg. She wore a partly opened blouse which exposed the fleshy top half of each of her breasts and her body reeked of cheap perfume.

What a sleaze, Bud thought.

"Hi guys! Drinks for the house," the Admiral announced.

Bud wondered, as he often had, where the Admiral got all of his money. The old man had never shared much of his background with patrons of the bar and what little he had was somewhat suspect. Questions lingered in Bud's mind: *Who was the Admiral? Where did he get all of his money? Was he really a seaman? What was his real background?*

A new entertainer was setting up, getting ready to begin his set on the small stage near the back of the pub.

"Hi ya'all my name's Hal and I'm here to entertain ya."

The greeting snapped Bud's attention away from his speculation about the Admiral. His interest turned to the stage.

"Where ya'all from? California? Alaska? Idaho? Canada? Welcome to our show. Any of you here to buy a condo? I'm thinking of going into real estate. My band members are going to be my salesmen."

"Hey you here to sing? Or are you selling time shares?" blurted Ben.

"Me and my band are here to drink sips and pick up tips. Let me introduce you to my band." Hal pointed to a solitary console which emitted sounds designed to enhance the music from his guitar.

"On the drums we have my brother Hull." The flip of a switch produced a drum roll at this announcement. "Next we have my other brother Hill on the keyboard." Bars from a keyed rendition of *Nine to Five* came from the console. "On the bass we have my third brother, Hell." The pulsating rhythm from

It's a Rainy Night followed. "We're called the HAUIE Brothers. It sounds Hawaiian but it really stands for Hal, Hull, Hill and Hell."

"Hey Hal," the Admiral bellowed, "D'you know *Sweet Caroline?*"

"Wait till I check with my band." Hal began turning dials and fumbling with tapes on the console. "Yeah me and my band know that one," he responded.

The music was good. Hal had a rich voice with a fullness enhanced by the resonance of the room. The backup music from the console, comprised of his imaginary brothers, added depth to the sounds of his guitar.

"Hey Hal let me buy you and your band a drink." This offer from someone in the audience exemplified the quickness with which the room picked up on his light-hearted reference to the fictitious band. The patrons were in the mood for more of this silliness.

"They don't drink but I do. I'll have a B29 to lubricate my vocal cords."

"They look like a pretty wild bunch Hal. How d'you keep your band under control?"

"Easy. If they fool around I don't pay 'em. They're pretty good really. They don't drink, don't go on strike, and they come to work on time." He began a medley of Harry Belafonte songs next.

At that moment Pam walked into the bar and flung herself down next to Tina. She babbled excitedly about something none of the group at the table could understand. Her arms flailed wildly as she chattered faster and faster in Tina's ear. A wild glint shone in her eyes as she poured out her news. With Hal's music filling the room no one, including Tina, could hear a word she was saying.

Hal launched into *Don't Worry Be Happy* as the crowd became caught up in the good natured bantering. He was in the middle of a whistling part in the song when the console let loose.

Sccccreeeeeeech!

"Christ, my ears! I thought you had those guys under control," Mia yelled from her barstool.

Hal was quick to respond. "I knew you were all goin' to give me a rough time...With a crowd like this I'm goin' to have to leave for the washroom to get a hold on myself."

"Let's hear *Tiny Bubbles*," one of the crowd asked.

"You got to be kidding. If I do that request my band'll walk off." Following that comment he left for his break, heading in the direction of the washroom.

Suddenly Pam rushed out of the bar leaving Tina with a pained look on her face. She wiped her head and arm with a napkin and screwed up her nose.

"What's wrong? Pam say something to bug you?" asked Bud.

"Christ, no! I couldn't hear a word she said. She kept spitting all over me when she was talking. I'm going to the washroom. I may even have to go home to wash my hair."

Hal returned after the break and launched into his routine singing songs, playing with the audience and working his concept of an imaginary band.

Tina and Janice became more excited as time went on. Not because of the entertainment or the company, rather because Rick promised to drop by sometime in the afternoon. He didn't normally socialize with members of his audience since his time for work and relaxation didn't coincide with theirs – they were on holidays and he wasn't. After they had consumed several drinks and a good feed of Pu Pus the afternoon became early evening. It looked like Rick wasn't going to show.

"**There he is! There he is**!" Tina cried out excitedly.

Rick stood in the doorway and peered through the darkened room until his eyes settled on the party of four. In spite of all the years he had lived in Waikiki this was the first time Rick had been in this bar. He ambled over to the table and greeted them with his flashy smile.

"Hi y'all. And what have we here?"

"Sit down and have a drink."

"I'll just have a coke. I'm due on stage in a couple of hours and I don't want to get bombed before the audience does."

As he drew up a chair Rick's eyes skirted the room. He took in the surroundings – the tourists sipping Mai Tais, an entertainer strumming his guitar on stage, and the regulars sitting at the bar. His eyes momentarily focused on the figures at the bar. A sudden tension gripped the air as a figure at the bar glared directly back at him.

The steely eyes of the Admiral took aim at Rick and his face flushed and a cruel sneer formed on his lips. The old man was instantly transformed from a gregarious and easy going old man to a grotesque figure with a red face and thin, pale lips. Veins bulged from his forehead and his eyes conveyed hatred. As his features took on a sinister appearance, others in the bar noticed it immediately.

In contrast the blood drained from Rick's cheeks, leaving them deathly white, and the muscles in his stomach tightened. Time seemed suspended as he was momentarily paralyzed.

Sliding off the bar stool, the Admiral swung his arm toward the top of his right shoe – a knife flashed in his hand. The customers were mesmerized. Someone was going to be hurt.

"Christ, it's Thug!" Rick gasped. He bolted for the door and was lost in the crowd on the street before the Admiral made it half way across the room.

CHAPTER 9

Back to the Beach

The driving rain pelted down with a vengeance. Sheets of water converged on the road below; rebounding off the pavement on impact and adding a significant contribution to the torrents of water streaming down the streets. Here and there kids skimmed the surface on bogey boards shrieking with delight as the warm deluge beat against their faces. The squall gained in fury as the wind whipped the downpour into a frenzy, lashing out in all directions.

From their viewpoint on the lanai Tina and Bud watched in dismay as their beach time dissolved in the surge. They both wore bathing suits, having prepared earlier for a foray to the beach. Tina wore the pink and white one with tassels on the side. It was her favorite; the tassels made her feel alive and vibrant when they rippled gently in the breeze. The vivid contrast of pink and white had the effect of a beacon drawing attention from a mile away on the beach. She loved attention and the suit facilitated it for her.

Bud, on the other hand, wore his favorite blue suit with white stripes on the side. He was partial to that bathing suit since he thought it made him look slim; it nicely covered the paunch beginning to form around his waistline. The beach mats were rolled and the towels, suntan lotion, pin money and watches were stored in the beach bag. Only a few minutes ago they had applied generous portions of lotion to their bodies. They were all greased up with gear in tow and all set to go. Now this!

"Damn it look at it Bud! We're all ready and now the sun's disappeared."

"Aw don't worry. It'll blow over soon. Look at those clouds move. Blue sky'll be here any minute."

"I hope so. We're almost through our holiday and need all the beach time we can get. We can have all the rain we want back in Seattle."

The couple settled into chairs on the lanai making the best of their situation by observing the show on the street below. The kids had disappeared, replaced by figures running from one doorway to the next; some with newspapers over their heads, others taking no precautions and resigning themselves to a drenching. The latter group did not seem overly concerned since the rain was warm and friendly.

A half hour passed with no letup in sight. By now the streets were deserted except for some cars sloshing their way through rain slicked roads. It seemed the day would be better suited for reading in the unit rather than lying on the beach.

"Look! Look! Blue sky's beginning to show over the water."

"Yeah and there's a rainbow over to the right."

A beautiful rainbow formed as the rain quickly receded into the distance. Shades of red, green and gold emerged, set in a backdrop of clear blue sky. The rainbow quickly grew in size and vividness of color as it arched its way across the sky. It was gorgeous, a glamorous vision painted from the brush of the master.

The rain squall which arrived with such a vengeance just as quickly beat a hasty retreat, leaving behind the crispness of renewal. It was instantly replaced with the dazzling brilliance of tropical sunshine. This abrupt departure of dark rainclouds, followed by a sudden appearance of blue sky inset with fluffy white clouds, was common in Hawaii. The trade winds kept the sky in constant turmoil. Each day they brought a mixture of clouds, rain and sunshine, none of which, with the exception of sunshine, usually stayed for very long.

"Beach time! Roll the wagons. Yo!"

The Toppers hit the beach in record time but not soon enough to beat hoards of others. Pam and Alice had already staked their claim and set up shop by the time the couple arrived. Tina made her way directly to them while Bud hung back a little taking his usual conservative stance in that section of beach. He was never sure whether the old ladies would welcome him or not. Bud felt they tolerated him only on the perimeter of their domain and for safety's sake he didn't venture into the inner recesses.

The old ladies were preoccupied when Tina arrived. With necks craned and fingers pointing they nodded at Tina, gesturing toward the figure of a man who had suddenly gained a great deal of attention. People were staring and pointing at him. Even passersby who could see him from the sidewalk stopped and stared. Cars honked their horns and people waved.

What the hell's going on? Tina thought as she glanced in that direction.

Through the onlookers she could barely make out the features of the man who was the focus of attention. Initially all she could see was the back of his head followed by a partial side profile. He wore dark sunglasses and his features were hauntingly familiar.

His long jet black hair extended down the sides of his face forming thick sideburns that fell just short of mutton chops. He had high cheekbones that suggested a hint of Indian blood from some time in the past. As he turned slightly toward her direction she could make out more; the finely chiseled features of his face, his pert nose and the slightly crooked smile on his face. All of a sudden recognition hit her like a ton of bricks!

"My God it's Elvis! Bud it's Elvis!"

"He's dead. It's just a guy who looks like him."

"No it's not, it's him! I've been reading those stories and they say he still lives. What do you think Pam?"

"Maybe tis and maybe tisn't. Just as long as the bum doesn't try t' muscle in on my section of beach."

Just then Janice appeared with Ben in tow, running pell-mell down the beach. Her arms jerked wildly as, with amazing deftness, she jumped to the left and right over prostrate figures lying every which way on the sand. She darted in and out of those beachgoers who were standing and staring in Elvis' direction.

"Guess what! Guess what!" she panted, caught up in the excitement of the moment.

"What?" Bud queried.

"I said guess you dummy! You didn't guess. Now guess!"

"Okay! I guess that Elvis is sun tanning on the beach."

"Now you've ruined my surprise. How did you guess? Ben did you tell everyone my surprise? I heard a rumor he was down here. I wonder where he is."

"He's right over there. We can see him from here."

"Where? Where? Where is he?"

"There. He's over there."

"Where? Where? Ohhhh! There he is guys, there he is... I saw him first!"

"Janice we've been watching him for the last ten minutes. He's been over there all along."

"Yeah. Sure, spoil my surprise again Bud. You always do."

In spite of the attention he generated no one had attempted to speak to Elvis. Instead, people just stared.

"Why doesn't somebody talk to him? Cum'on Janice let's go talk to him," Tina suggested.

The two women sauntered over toward their idol.

"Hi Elvis! My name's Tina and this is my friend Janice."

Elvis acknowledged the greeting with a smile and a nod of his head but said nothing. Two hefty looking men sitting nearby moved toward the women as they approached him. Noticing the sudden movement of the men, Tina and Janice kept their distance. There was no use in provoking them if they were Elvis' bodyguards.

"Nice seeing you Elvis. Have a nice day."

Elvis smiled in acknowledgement and they returned to their spot on the beach.

"He acknowledged us. I'm so excited," Janice announced.

"Don't be a dummy," Ben said, "He's not Elvis."

"He is too. So take off! I wonder why he didn't say anything."

"They say his voice went," Pam offered. "Maybe that's why they had a fake funeral and why he didn't answer you."

"What a pile of garbage. Elvis is dead."

"He is not! Stop ruining everything."

Shortly afterward the two couples decided to leave the beach for the rest of the afternoon. On the way past the celebrity the women once again wished him good day. Elvis smiled and nodded in their direction.

* * * * * *

The next day they returned once again to the beach. Tina was anxious to see if Elvis would be there. Sure enough he was there large as life.

"Hi Elvis remember me? I'm Tina."

Elvis smiled in return and waved a greeting. The two hefty men were there again keeping vigil. The Toppers continued their journey toward Pam and Alice's turf.

"Do you really think that could be Elvis?" Tina asked Pam.

"Could be."

"I wonder why he doesn't talk?"

"I told you yesterday. They say his voice went and that's why the funeral was faked. I read it in the *Enquirer.*"

At that moment Rocco appeared. He shifted his balance from foot to foot as he threaded his way along the beach, ready to move in a flash in any direction if necessary. He sniffed the air for danger, like a wild animal, as his eyes darted back and forth looking for some real or imagined adversary. Eventually he noticed Bud and with a nod of recognition began moving toward him. Midway towards Bud he spotted Elvis and stopped abruptly. Without missing a beat he spun around one hundred and eighty degrees and beat the hell out of there.

"Bud what happened to Rocco? One minute he's on his way over and the next he disappears."

"I don't know. It looked like he spotted someone he wanted to avoid."

"Oh well let's enjoy our beach time. I don't care for him anyway. By the way, here comes Janice and Ben."

"Hi guys. I see Elvis is here again. I tried to talk to him but he didn't speak."

"They say his voice went," Pam offered, in imitation of a broken record.

"Can you imagine? Elvis on our beach. It's so exciting! I wonder why he won't speak?" Janice pondered, ignoring Pam's comment.

"Dammit! I told you his voice went!" Pam growled. "I read it in the *Enquirer*."

"Let's try to talk to him again Janice. I'll take a picture of you with him."

"Oh sure. Tina. If he says no. I'm the one who's embarrassed, not you."

"Don't be so sensitive. If he says no at least he'll have said something."

"His voice went dammit! I told you his voice went! I read it." By this time Pam's eyes blazed and her nostrils flared. She began stamping her foot and pawing the sand like a stallion ready to do battle. She didn't like to be ignored, especially when it happened on her own turf.

"Oh dry up Pam!" Tina commanded. "Okay Janice let's go."

The women shifted their way across the sand until they confronted Elvis. The two hefty men were nowhere in sight. Were they his bodyguards or just two sunbathers who had no involvement with him?

"Hi Elvis! It's us again. Remember? I'm Tina and this is Janice."

The man nodded in greeting, saying nothing.

"Can I take your picture with Janice? The camera's all set."

Elvis shook his head from side to side but said nothing.

Tina ignored the negative response. "Why won't you talk? If you don't say anything I'm taking your picture anyway."

The determined tone in Tina's voice made it clear to Elvis that she was going to take his picture whether he wanted it or not. He tried to wave her off but to no avail.

"Well what do you say? Are you going to speak or do we shoot?"

Elvis' face reddened as he struggled with the demand. The veins in his neck stood out and his mouth began to quiver as he attempted to respond. With a shrug of his shoulders a smirk formed on his face. Finally he tipped his head and made a sweeping bow as he responded.

"Blimey mates o'im not E'vis. M'name's Oinee. Oinee Mc'ellar at yer service. An 'ow can oi 'elp ya?"

* * * * *

Earlier Days - Ernie the Elvis Imitator

Ernie McKellar was raised just a stone's throw from the docks in Liverpool, England. He lived in the backyard of the famous Beatles rock group, the biggest export to hit Liverpool in decades. The Beatles were the toast of the city and the favorite of every teenager raised in Liverpool during the 60s, that is every teenager except Ernie McKellar. Ernie was a fervent Elvis fan in whose eyes no other performer could replace the King – not the Beatles, the Rolling Stones or any other group or single entertainer. The King was his idol! In fact Ernie thought Elvis was more godlike than king!

Ernie tried to emulate Elvis in any way he could. While still in his teens he grew long hair and sideburns and wore clothes patterned after his idol. In those days he hadn't yet begun to shave regularly and consequently found it difficult to grow a decent pair of sideburns. To compensate he used his mother's mascara to supplement the little hair he was able to cultivate on his cheeks. This embellishment worked well at a distance but was less effective from close up. His costume consisted of tight jeans, flashy shirts with interwoven metallic thread, and white bucks. He threw the white bucks away, however, when some idiot asked if he was trying to impersonate Pat Boone.

By watching Elvis' rare appearances on TV and by studying his mannerisms over and over again in the movies Ernie was able to perfect his imitation of the master. He developed a slight tick in his face and frequently moved his head from left to right, in imitation of moves made by Elvis when singing *Jailhouse Rock*. He also managed to master the famous smile formed by raising his top lip at a slight angle.

While listening to his own rendition of *Don't Be Cruel* as he practiced singing in the bathroom, Ernie thought he sounded exactly like Elvis. However, whenever he attempted to sing in any other location, without the resonance of the bathroom and the musical backup from the record, his impression fell far short of perfection. This shortfall was painfully apparent when he performed at a public function for the first and last time.

Ernie's eventful performance took place during half time at a soccer match attended by over 5000 fans. He didn't really want to make a first public appearance in front of such a large audience but his friends at the pub had dared him to prove he could perform in front of strangers. Prior to this commitment he had been boasting about how good his imitations were getting. In response, one of his mates bet him twenty pounds he was too chicken to perform at a public event. Ernie took the bet and agreed to perform anywhere he was asked. Little did he know it would be in front of such a large and potentially hostile audience. One of the regulars at the pub knew the stadium manager and told him Ernie was an up and coming professional who would provide the fans with a special entertainment treat.

Now the time of reckoning was near. Ernie slouched on a rickety old chair in the dark and dingy change room. A musty smell of stale sweat and urine hung close in the dead air. He dreaded the call to perform. His nerves were tied in knots and an empty sensation settled into the pit of his stomach. The cold sweat on his forehead and hands added to his discomfort. What if they didn't like him? What if he made a fool of himself? It was one thing to be viewed as an idiot in front of a roomful of friends, quite another to earn that dubious distinction in front of thousands of strangers.

A roar from the crowd penetrated the little room as a whistle sounded the end of the first half. He could hear the announcement of half time entertainment over the public address system.

"**Ladies and gentlemen we have pulled out all stops to provide you with an absolutely spectacular half time show. We have booked the best there is. You are in for the treat of your lives**."

There was no response from the crowd. Either they didn't hear the announcement or couldn't care less.

God don't overdo it, Ernie found himself thinking. *I shouldn't even be here let alone part of a so-called spectacular show. I'll probably be the only klutz in the line-up.*

Why did he let himself get suckered into this? It was insane. How could he get out of this? He felt slightly nauseous. If he got sick would that be an out? God, if he could die he would.

"Now ladies and gentlemen, our first act will be by a new and fabulous imitator of Rich Little. He will absolutely astound you with his larger than life imitations. **Ladies and Gentlemen, put your hands together for the great 'Little Richey'!"**

A few catcalls greeted the performer. Most ignored the introduction – intent on getting beer from the concession stands as quickly as possible.

Little Richey bowed toward the audience and immediately launched into his act. He imitated sounds of trains, planes and car engines by breathing and growling directly into the mike. Before he got to his race car imitation the crowd whistled and booed him off the stage.

He was a disaster!

The announcer quickly introduced the next act. He was anxious to get the audience's mind off Little Richey before the scene turned ugly.

This time no fanfare preceded the announcement as he introduced Ralph the wonder dog. Ralph was an old corgi mutt who was supposed to sing *God Save the Queen*. After several unsuccessful attempts to get the dog to utter a sound, some members of the crowd began to bark. The barking picked up momentum until it drowned out any sound from the stage. With a display of annoyance the dog's owner packed Ralph off the stage, accompanied by booing from the crowd and a shower of empty beer cans.

Finally, it was Ernie's turn!

Ernie had waited a long time for his first public appearance. Now he was petrified with fright. His plan had been to play a record of Elvis singing *Hound Dog* in the background. He would lip-synch the words and add the appropriate facial contortions and hip gyrations.

The exasperated master of ceremonies, still reeling from the crowd's rude response to the earlier acts, attempted to lay a guilt trip on the audience. They weren't in the mood.

"Ladies and gentlemen we are about to see a young and rising star who you will think is the real thing. Please grant him the respect he so richly deserves. I beg of you, act as mature ladies and gentlemen. Having said that it is with great pleasure that I bring you Ernie McKellar, the next Elvis, singing *Hound Dog*".

The music blared from the speakers as Ernie dressed in his tight costume and wearing his best Elvis look launched into the song. The crowd started in before he finished the first bar.

"Bring back the other hound dog and see if it'll sing this time," someone bellowed.

"You never caught a rabbit and you ain't no friend of mine," Ernie lip-synched.

"Ya ain't no friend o' mine either Oinie," another yelled.

By this time the crowd began foot stamping and barking. It didn't matter who the entertainer was. They were having none of it. The noise became deafening. Ernie's eyes bulged out of his sockets as the movement of his lips slowed to a dead stop. His back up music over the public address system was lost in the roar of the crowd.

It was time to leave!

Ernie sprang from the stage – guitar in hand. The seat of his pants split wide open as he bounded down the steps. The crowd loved it. They sent him off amid catcalls and dog barks, and a thunderous cheer rang out as he finally disappeared under the stands. It was a disastrous debut. One that wasn't conducive to fond memories.

After that experience Ernie decided that show business was not for him. He contented himself as an Elvis look-a-like but not as an impressionist. Over the subsequent years he basked in the adoration heaped upon him by Elvis fans and chose to say nothing at all as he feared his Cockney accent would detract from the illusion.

CHAPTER 10

The Maui Experience

"Wake up! Wake up! C'mon Bud wake up!"

Tina pounded him repeatedly on his back. A hollow sound emanated from deep within the cavity of his chest adding a resonance to the thumps. At the start she shook his shoulder with her left hand, placed her right hand on his forehead and rotated his head from side to side. When he ignored this technique the rhythmic pounding began.

"**I said wake up, dammit! I know you're awake.**"

"Mmmmmmmmmmmph!"

"Bud I know you're awake! Now get up!"

"Christ what time is it?" he mumbled sleepily.

"It's 5:00 A.M. already."

"What! How come you're up at this ungodly hour? I'm going back to sleep." Bud rolled sideways and pulled the cover over his head. Then he plunked the pillow on top for good measure.

"**No you don't! Get up! Get up!**" Tina supplemented her demand by yanking the cover off the bed and onto the floor. To augment her authority she began to hit Bud in the head with a pillow.

"Awright! Awright! I give up! Now, what's the big deal why did you drag me out of bed in the middle of the night?"

"It's not the middle of the night and if that's your attitude then I'm not going to tell you."

"What? You yank me out of bed at an ungodly hour and now you're not going to tell me why?"

"Piss off!"

"Tell me!"

"No! Not unless you're going to listen objectively to what I'm going to say."

"Okay! I'm objective! Now what's the big news?"

"You're not objective."

"Am too."

"No you're not!"

"Yes I am dammit! Now what were you going to say?"

Tina's eyes sparkled as her mind wrapped itself around her predetermined plan. She had waited to get his attention and to arouse his curiosity before she sprung it on him. Quickly now, and while he was still in a daze she must be proactive. "We're going to Maui! I'll phone the Whites and the airline."

"What d'you mean we're going to Maui? No way! I want to rest right here. We only have two days left in our vacation. Forget it."

"Bud I really want to go to Maui. Please. Let's take a flight out this morning. I won't ask you for anything else if you take me." Tina changed her tactics mid-stream once she had heard Bud's initial reaction to the idea.

"Forget it! I'm going back to bed."

She could tell her approach so far wasn't working. Bud dove back under the covers leaving her frustrated and alone at the edge of the bed. Now it was time to switch to her back-up plan. She marched over to the telephone and dialed Janice's number.

"Janice? Did I get you out of bed?... Sorry! It's time you were up anyway. I have this great idea. Bud likes it too. Why don't we go to Maui for an overnight trip?"

A puzzled, silent reaction greeted her suggestion. Undaunted Tina proceeded with her one way conversation.

"...Why not?

"Well **YOU** asked why and I can just as easily ask why not.

"… Okay, okay … it's because it would be fun to visit another island for a change... that's why."

Tina got the impression that Janice was warming to the idea as the response at the other end of the phone began to sound more positive. Her friend's initial reaction was probably due to a sleepy state of mind. Now was the time to strike, acting in a firm and decisive way.

"Okay Janice. I've already booked space for the four of us. Bud's dying to go and Ben will love it. Besides it will give him a chance to get away from that creepy Rocco for a change. You'd like that wouldn't you? ... Alright you work on Ben while I get everything ready to go.

"...Good! We'll catch the 10:00 A.M. flight and be at Lahaina well before lunch time. Aren't you excited? I can hardly wait.

"... and don't worry Janice! Once you wake up you'll be more excited than I am. See you out front in a cab at exactly 8 o'clock... Bye!"

After hanging up Tina launched into action. First, a call to Hawaiian Air to book four places on the 10 o'clock flight, with a return the following evening. Next, a call to arrange for a car and two sleeping units at Lahaina. After making the arrangements she was left with one minor detail...Bud.

She decided to pack their bags next. Bud would appreciate her initiative. If all the arrangements were made—bags packed and the Whites going—he would be receptive to the idea. After all, she thought, he seemed more annoyed with missing his sleep than at the idea of the trip. Timing, however, was crucial so she waited until 7:00 before her next move.

"Bud honey, it's 7:00. Time you were up," Tina cooed. "Coffee's ready and the eggs'll be done in two minutes."

Slowly and lazily Bud gradually stirred in the sack stretching his arms and legs to their full extent. God it felt good! He yawned and slowly rolled off the bed and onto the floor. He lay there for a minute caressed by the lushness of the carpet.

Bud was pleasantly surprised about Tina's up beat tone of voice. Usually she pouted when she didn't get her way. There was no point in raising the issue with her again since she was probably resolved to staying in Waikiki.

What a hair-brained idea anyway, he thought to himself. *Imagine wanting to go to Maui on the spur of the moment and with only two days left in the holiday.*

He sauntered over to the dining table and sat down, a contented look on his face. He reached for the coffee cup Tina held out and drank in the rich aroma of freshly brewed coffee. Bacon sizzled on the stove lending a sweet, lightly smoked maple sugar fragrance to the room. His stomach rumbled in anticipation of the mouth watering fare he was about to receive.

Ahhhhhh! – life couldn't be better.

"Better hurry and eat hon! We haven't much time before we leave."

"Leave? Leave for where? Are we going somewhere?"

"Yes. I thought you agreed. Janice and Ben are dying to go to Maui and have already made all the arrangements. We don't want to disappoint them do we?"

"Disappoint them? What about me? I'll be bloody disappointed if we leave Waikiki. Tell them to forget it. We're not going!"

"But Bud all the arrangements are made. If we cancel it will cost you the price of a night at the hotel in Lahaina on your credit card."

"What? You already booked with my card? What the hell's going on?"

"Don't be such a snot! Janice and Ben will be waiting for us in a cab downstairs in thirty minutes. We're all packed. Now eat your breakfast while I floss my teeth."

The thought of paying for a night's accommodation they may not use had a sobering effect on Bud's attitude toward the trip. Besides if Ben and Janice were so anxious to go it might be fun and something different to do for a change. Five years had passed since they last visited Maui. It would be interesting to see what changes had taken place in that time.

He wolfed down his breakfast and rinsed the dishes in the sink. Shortly afterward they arrived downstairs, carrying their beach mats and overnight bag. The taxi with Ben and Janice inside waited at the front of the complex.

Janice's face was beaming. She had accepted the trip and was excited about visiting the outer island. Ben, on the other hand, sat there with a somber look on his face.

"Hi guys. All set to go?" Tina greeted.

"Can't wait! We're really excited. Right Ben?" Janice responded.

"Yeah," Ben replied unenthusiastically.

The women jabbered incessantly on the way to the airport. Once in awhile a question was directed at one of the husbands – each time it received a curt, subdued response.

"You know Bud, I hope you appreciate this. The only reason I'm going on this trip is because you wanted to go so badly," Ben confided.

"What are you crazy? The only reason I'm going is because you thought it was so urgent!" Bud shot back.

Then it suddenly clicked. Both men looked at each other knowingly, shrugged their shoulders, and resigned themselves to this last minute side trip to another island.

To help smooth things over Tina had made car rental arrangements with the company that advertised the cheapest rates in the Waikiki Beach Press. It would be only $19.95 for twenty-four hours. She proudly announced the special price to Bud on the plane trip over hoping to cheer him up.

As soon as they deplaned in Kahului, Bud raced over to the car rental booth. It was one of several outlets located at the airport. At the front of each were several people waiting to complete rental transactions. Finally his turn came.

"Topper. We have a reservation. You know, your $19.95 special," Bud announced.

"Yes, Mr. Topper. We have a car ready for you. Would you like full insurance coverage? It includes hubcap insurance."

"What the hell is hubcap insurance? I'm going to be driving a car, not a hubcap."

"Well it's up to you. We've had some problems with hub cap thefts and the deductible is $500 if you don't want full coverage."

"How much is full coverage?"

"It's $18."

"For a week? We only have the car for twenty-four hours."

"No. It's $18 for twenty-four hours."

"Christ! That's as much as the whole car costs to rent. This is highway robbery!"

"It's the going rate. Would you like full coverage or not?"

"Hell, no! Ben! Take those hubcaps off. We'll throw 'em in the trunk."

Eventually they were underway. The men in the front seat, the women in the back, and the hubcaps in the trunk.

"Look Janice! The coastline is beautiful. Aren't you glad we came?" Tina posed.

"It's exciting. I can hardly wait 'til we get to Lahaina. The beach nearby at Kaanapali is supposed to be out of this world."

"What do you guys think? Aren't you glad we made you come?"

Both men reluctantly nodded in agreement. Actually the trip didn't seem like such a bad idea after all. Bud and Ben both began to look forward to the rest of it. In particular they were anxious to get to the beach to report for bikini patrol.

After a three hour drive the two couples arrived at the hotel which Tina had booked that morning. It looked acceptable on the outside at least. However, it had probably seen better days. It was noticeable that the carpet in the hallway was threadbare and the walls needed a good scrubbing. They found the rooms to be Spartan in appearance but serviceable, after all they would spend little time in them since they planned to sight see and lay on the beach as much as possible.

"Meet you on the beach in twenty minutes Janice."

"Okay Tina. By the way, you can bring Bud along if you want. I'm thinking of bringing my grouch with me too. Of course neither of them wanted to come in the beginning."

The beach was beautiful. Snow white sand stretched for miles along the shore. It was bordered on one side by lush green grass and huge palm trees swaying slowly in the gentle breeze. On the other side the sun danced off the sparkling blue water, lending its brilliance to the vivid colors. Waves crashed onto the beach and rushed along its perimeter before retreating back into the ocean's depths amid froth, foam and assorted debris.

"Look at those surfers bobbing around out there," Tina exclaimed. "They must be skilful and brave to ride those little boards on such big waves. I'll bet both Bud and Ben couldn't do that, right Janice?"

"Right."

"Oh yeah! Those guys are prob'ly a bunch of dummies out there. Can you imagine, sitting around all day, bobbing up and down like a doughnut in a cup of coffee? It don't take any skill or brains to do that. Right Ben?"

"Right Bud – piece of cake."

"Listen Bud if you're so bloody smart let's see you do it," Tina piped in.

"No way. It's so easy it would be an insult to my athletic talents."

"Bull! You're chicken and you know it."

"Am not!"

"Don't give us that garbage. You're chicken."

"Alright I'll show you peasants how it's done. Coming Ben?"

"No. Go 'head, I'll watch from here."

Bud walked over to the rental shack on the edge of the beach and picked out a bright and shiny red model. It would be easier for the others to see when he rode it in on the rollers. He placed the end of the surfboard on the beach and tipped it from side to side, peering in the direction of the others. This gesture was intended to gain their undivided attention before he plunged into the surf and out to where the big ones lurked. It didn't matter that he had never been on a surfboard before – it looked simple enough. Any dummy could do it. After all he had ice and roller skated as a kid. Surely he could stand up on a two by eight foot piece of wood.

As he arrived at the water's edge he gingerly laid the surfboard on the sand. Just then a big wave rolled in. It picked up the board and flung it up on the beach with Bud in hot pursuit. No sooner did he reach the board's new location than the return swell dragged it back out again into the water. He shifted gears quickly, following it into the surf.

"Good move Bud! Such an expert! You can't even capture the damn thing!" Tina shouted from her vantage point.

Bud had no time to respond to such trivial comments. He was intent on apprehending his bright red surfboard before it seriously ruined his credibility as a surfer.

Before he could reach it the next wave brought the board flying back up the beach. As it reached the level he stood at, Bud lunged at it! "Got 'cha, you little bastard!" he yelled at the board as he grabbed the end of it. Now he would show them! The next thing was to straddle the board, lie face down on it, and paddle beyond the crashing surf near the beach, out to where the other surfers bobbed in the swells. Now he was back in control. The rest would be a snap.

He jumped on the board, feet dangling on either side, and promptly turned a somersault in the water. He was completely submerged as the next wave carried him and the upside down board all the way back up to the top of the beach.

"What happened Bud, did it buck you off?" Janice taunted.

"No I think he's showing all his expert 'hot dog' tricks before beginning any serious surfing," Tina added gleefully.

"**Buggar off**!" he shouted at them before returning to the attack. He chased the board out into the surf before it was flung back again on the return swell. Each time it avoided his clutch. This was getting embarrassing! He couldn't even get off the bloody beach.

Finally, on the next attempt, he caught the board and somehow got it past the crest of the waves. However, rather than paddling it out in the normal fashion he had to resort to pushing it in front of him while kicking his feet for propulsion – not very professional looking, but he had to get away from the beach at any cost in order to avoid the jeers and taunts. Now at least he had made it out to where the water was deep enough so big rollers couldn't pick him up and slam him back onto the sand.

Bobbing about while out with the pros rekindled his confidence. Before attempting to ride one of the big swells, however, he decided to closely observe how the others did it. It was important that he do it right the first time in an attempt to salvage his pride. It looked simple enough. Now he was ready to try.

First he waved shoreward, in the hope that Tina and the Whites could see him clearly enough. As he waved they waved back. Good! They could see him. Now he would show them.

Bud spotted a big one coming his way! He grabbed the board with both hands and was ready to spring aboard in order to ride it in, while standing erect. Just before the wave hit, Bud leapt onto the board, prepared for action. He was immediately flipped end-over-end and into the water as the board overturned. Imagine, wiped out even before the wave arrived. Cheers and laughter greeted him from the beach. A second attempt and then a third yielded the same results.

To hell with it! Surfing was for the birds. What kind of a dumb sport was it anyway when they rented out faulty boards? Bud decided to paddle back to shore and accept the kidding he knew would come.

Coming in proved easier than going out. He made it to the beach with little difficulty and returned the board to the rental shack.

"Back already?" the attendant queried.

"Bloody right. You must have rented me a broken board. It wouldn't stay upright."

The attendant smiled at this comment. He had seen this happen with tourists over and over again. They didn't realize that it took skill and practice just to stand on a surfboard let alone to ride it in on the crest of a wave.

With his pride wounded Bud returned to where the others stood. His mind flashed over all of the recent events searching for excuses to parry the thrusts coming his way.

"Well the great surfer returns. How was it Bud? You put on an impressive display!" Tina greeted.

"Piss off! The board was broken. Okay?"

"How could the board be broken? It doesn't have any moving parts."

"I told you it was broken. The keel was missing or something. How can you keep it upright without a keel? Now let's change the subject."

The three could tell by the tone in Bud's voice that further kidding would not be well received. They wisely decided to discuss other matters.

"Let's go for a drink," Ben suggested.

"Yeah we should try that peanut bar I've heard about," Janice suggested. "I just love peanuts and they give you all you can eat."

"I haven't a clue where it is," Ben chipped in. "Why don't we just go to one nearby?"

"I want to go to the peanut bar!" Janice demanded.

After a lengthy search they found the tavern. It was pitch black inside. The contrast between the dazzling sunshine outside and the darkness of the bar left them temporarily blinded. They felt their way over to a table, occasionally bumping into people or objects along the way.

"**Take your hand off my face buddy!**" a voice threatened in the darkness.

"Sorry," Ben replied. "Just trying to get my bearings."

"**Well get 'em somewhere else!**"

"Here's a table! Here's a table!" Janice cried excitedly. "Isn't this neat? Like having a drink in the inner sanctum."

"Oh sure it's neat alright. But it's more like drinking in the basement with the lights out," Bud replied sarcastically.

"Don't be such a party pooper Bud," Tina jumped in. "This is fun and you better enjoy it."

"Where're the peanuts?" Ben asked.

"In the bowl on the table. They're all in shells. God but they're good." Janice began feeding her face before she even sat down.

"Oh gross I can even feel shells on the floor under my feet," Tina announced. "Some people are sure sloppy. Can you imagine dropping shells on the floor?"

"This bowl is full of empty shells," Ben cried out. "Let's call the waiter to replace it."

"Okay! Hey waiter! Four Mai Tais and a bowl of nuts!" Bud called out.

"I can't get over these shells on the floor. Some people are sure messy," Tina repeated.

The waiter arrived with the drinks and a heaping bowl of peanuts. He was offered the bowl of empty shells in return. Nonchalantly the waiter just dumped them on the floor and walked off with the empty bowl.

"Look! Look! The waiter is just dumping the shells on the floor," Tina called out. "I can't get over it."

"Well isn't that neat," Bud responded. "Might attract cockroaches though."

"Cockroaches! Did you say cockroaches?" Tina blurted a sudden panic in her voice.

"Yeah. Who knows in this darkness there could be all kinds of them crawling around on the floor. They might even climb into your sandals."

"Let's get the hell out of here!" Tina shrieked.

"But we haven't finished our drinks," Bud pleaded.

"Who cares! I'm getting out of here. Coming Janice?"

"Yeah! What a dump! Whose idea was it t'come here anyway? Yours Ben?"

The drinks sat on the table, unfinished, as the foursome with the women in the lead charged out of the premises.

"Let's try that bar over by the pool," Tina suggested.

The bar was located at the bottom of a set of stairs located adjacent to a swimming pool. As the couples descended down the stairway they entered into a unique setting. It was an underwater bar, decorated with a marine motif, in which patrons could gain a below the surface view of swimmers in the pool. The entire wall behind the bartender was made of transparent Plexiglas providing visual access to the scene.

"Look!" Janice exclaimed. "Isn't that something Ben? You can see underneath all of the swimmers and even the bubbles they make when they dive in. Isn't that neat?"

"Yeah. But I wonder whether the swimmers know we can see them?"

"Probably not. That's what makes it more interesting," Bud added.

They ordered drinks and sat back to watch the show. About a dozen swimmers of all different shapes and sizes were visible behind the bar. Some were floating on their backs, others swam lazily on the surface and one or two dove repeatedly into the water.

"See the bubbles which form when they dive in? It looks neat. Right Bud?"

Bud ignored Tina's question as his attention focused elsewhere.

"I said don't the bubbles look neat? Quit ignoring me Bud. What are you staring at anyway?"

In response Bud pointed in the direction of his interest. It centered on a woman by herself at the deep end of the pool. She had removed the bottom of her bikini and was innocently treading water in what she thought was complete privacy.

"I'm conducting research," he explained. "Hmm, I thought she was a blonde but I see she's really a brunette. Hey Ben this is better than the peanut bar isn't it?"

Ben was ready with a smart-assed reply. However he held back on it when he noticed the icy stare Janice directed his way. Instead his response was much more subdued. "Not bad scenery and there aren't any cockroaches around either."

"To hell with you guys. Let's drink up and go back to the beach," Tina suggested.

"How come?" Bud asked. "You don't swim and you don't like to wade where there are big waves."

"I'm goin' to go in. Just give me a chance to get used to it. And no smart remarks or I'll blab about your surfboarding all over Seattle."

Upon their return to the beach the women refused to go anywhere near the water. Instead they preferred to sit on the sand and gossip. After several dips in the ocean Bud became frustrated.

"Aw come on Tina. Give it a try. You only have to go up to your knees."

"Yeah. Easy for you to say. You can swim."

"Come on. There's nothing to worry about."

"Forget it."

"Listen you dragged me here. The least you can do is get your knees wet."

"Oh, all right. I'll go in for a minute. But you got to hold my hand in case a big wave comes." Tina moved gingerly in the direction of the ocean. The coolness of the surf felt pleasing as the waves lapped against her legs on their way up the beach and tugged gently against them on return. It felt refreshing, a welcome contrast to the heat of the sun which beat on the sand.

"Now isn't this fun? You've got to admit it."

"Yeah I guess so. But don't go out any further, I don't want to drown."

"Come on you're only up to your ankles when the waves come in. At least go to your knees."

"If you insist but don't let go of my hand. I'm kind of scared, this water scares me."

"Don't be ridiculous. This is fun and you haven't even got your bathing suit wet."

Tina gained in courage as the waves came in and receded back, over and over again. She became frivolous, laughing as the sea tickled her knees on each trip. This really was fun she thought. She should have listened to Bud earlier.

The visit was becoming a real success. The women loved the beach and the men, who were reluctant at first, were really getting into the swing of it. Bud, in particular, was pleased that Tina had tricked him into going; in spite of the fact it took the threat of having to pay for an unused hotel room to finally convince him.

The afternoon wore on as they continued frolicking in the surf. Tina was in great spirits, waiting for each wave with anticipation. Suddenly a huge roller burst in unexpectedly! It picked both of them up in its fury as it crashed toward shore, thrusting each of them in opposite directions. They were picked up bodily, momentarily suspended on the wave's crest, and then tossed, like rag dolls onto the sand.

Tina emerged from the swell sputtering and cursing. The foam from the whitecap swirled around her legs as it quickly receded. Her bathing suit was heavy with sand as it drooped, perilously close to falling off. A piece of green seaweed trailed from her hair.

Her eyes blazed and her nostrils flared as she shook her fist menacingly in Bud's direction. His body was still caught up in the surf's fury as it rolled him over and over, like a football kicked end over end. The ocean's might had ripped his bathing suit off, tumbling it in the swell – a multi-colored rag, adding another ingredient to the mix of froth and seaweed brought in by the sea.

"You tried to kill me!" Tina screamed at Bud over the fray. "You asshole, you tried to kill me!"

By this time the sea had receded, leaving Bud lying in its wake, naked in the sand. He clung, face down, hugging the shore like a long lost friend – his rear exposed to the elements. Exposure of his bum, he reasoned, was of less cost to his dignity than the other options open to him.

Janice ran over to console Tina who by this time was busy shaking sand out of her suit. She had moved up the beach well out of the reach of the surf. It became Ben's job to help Bud out of his predicament. He slowly sauntered over to the prostrate figure with a towel in his hand.

"Well Bud maybe the two old ladies on Kuhio Beach couldn't rip your shorts off but King Neptune managed to."

"Never mind the cracks. Just give me the towel!"

Wrapped in the towel Bud dashed down the beach anxious to disappear from the view of the grinning onlookers. When he arrived where Tina and Janice stood he was met with an ultimatum.

"I want to go back to Waikiki!" Tina demanded.

"But we paid for the room tonight. We can't just pack up and leave."

"**I don't care! I'm going back to Waikiki... Now!**"

"You're the one who wanted to come here. You tricked me into coming and now I'm enjoying myself."

"**You tried to drown me**."

"Don't be ridiculous!"

"Janice and I are going back whether you two want to come or not! So there!"

Bud knew her mind was made up. He shrugged his shoulders and reluctantly followed her back to the room to pack. What a waste of money. The cost of airfare, a rental car used only for half a day and a hotel room which would be left vacant this evening, all for only a few hours on Maui. Bud felt sick.

Silence dominated the flight back to Honolulu. Both men were exasperated because of the early return and the waste of money. The women, on the other hand, were hostile to their husbands for another reason. They blamed Bud for the unexpected arrival of the huge wave and implicated Ben just for being his friend.

There was one bright spot, however. They would salvage a full day at the beach tomorrow. It was the last day of their holiday before the dreaded trip back home to Seattle. This time both couples were scheduled to leave on the same flight.

CHAPTER 11

The Puzzle With A New Twist

Kuhio Beach attracted an assortment of local characters who supplemented the throngs of beachgoers. They worked the seashore on a regular basis. Several times each day these individuals passed along the beach walk looking for goods or else delivering unsolicited messages.

This day was no different than others as the Toppers and Whites attempted to catch the last rays of sunshine before returning to Seattle the next morning. From their vantage point on the beach they watched the round of characters making their routine visits.

In the distance they noticed a bag lady shuffling along the sidewalk adjoining the beach. She was rummaging in garbage cans and sifting through the grass looking for bottles or other discarded items of value. This was one of several trips she made daily on her scavenging route. She was bundled in tattered, multi-colored clothing wrapped several layers deep around her body. Her toes and heels protruded through holes in the soiled running shoes tied to her feet. On her head was a floppy black hat with a veil that provided a measure of privacy from the stares of onlookers. Her padded presence, which would have been appropriate for the cold of a Chicago winter, contrasted sharply with the skimpy clothing worn by beachgoers.

In one hand she carried a green garbage bag containing the fruits of her labor. Her other hand grasped a long gnarled stick used to forage through the grass and to warn people and dogs to keep their distance.

Further down the beach the words of a wandering preacher could be heard above the sounds of the street:

"Repent ye sinners for the Lord is the way! Come away from the devil for ye worship the sun – not the Lord Jesus Christ."

The sunbathers ignored the message. They were at the beach to relax and to enjoy the warmth of the sun's rays, not to listen to a sermon from a self-proclaimed messiah.

"Listen oh ye sinners! Through me I can lead you to the glory land. I can show you the light. Why do you not repent? The book of Psalms gives

you the answer. **You are to lie in green pastures not on a hot beach."**

"Take off Mac! I'm here for the beach not Sunday school," a voice shouted from the throng.

"You! You who will not listen! Hear me! I have the answer."

"I said take off! Bother someone else or I'll give you MY answer."

Given this negative response delivered with such conviction, the preacher decided to press his way further along the beach. As he faded into the distance the Word could still be heard.

"...Repent ye sinners for the Lord is the way!"

The preacher would return with the same message on his afternoon round.

Next a tall skinny man with a peculiar gait appeared on the scene. He carried a wand that was attached to a set of headphones he wore on his bald head. With a rhythmic sweeping motion he examined parts of the beach with his wand that were not occupied either by sunbathers or beach gear. With the metal detector he searched for loose change or jewelry left behind by careless beachgoers.

"Beep... beep... beep!"

The machine produced this sound whenever it located something of interest. As soon as the sound was emitted the scrawny man would quickly rake the sand with a strainer in search of some anticipated treasure. Usually nothing of value was found – a pull tab from a pop or beer can, for example, could cause it to beep.

The treasure hunter made this trek each morning on a predetermined route. He adjusted the time of day, however, to coincide with low tide. When he was on this section of the beach he took great care to cut a wide swathe around the territory claimed by Pam and Alice. He was aware of their reputation.

"Pape! ... Paaaaaape!"
The cry of a newspaper hawker broke the serenity of the beach almost every half hour. Usually it was a young boy out to make a few dollars selling papers to tourists. Since tenure under the hot sun was short, frequent returns were made by the hawkers in an attempt to sell papers to new arrivals at the beach.

After watching the daily parade Tina grew restless. It was the last day before returning home and she had grown tired of the familiar visitors. Besides she was somewhat irritable at the thought of returning to the dampness and cold of Seattle.

"Let's get the hell out of here! We haven't finished our shopping anyway. Whad'ya say Janice, ready to go?"

"Why not? Ben's as red as Santa's outfit anyway. Let's go."

* * * * *

A shopping center was the last place Bud wanted to be on the final day of his vacation. Tina had insisted that he go with her to carry parcels. He had agreed reluctantly, not because he was willing to carry parcels but rather to keep Tina's spending in line. Left to her own devices she would ravage his credit card accounts. The men quickly grew tired of following their wives from one department to another at each of the stores in the mall. Not only did they pay an initial visit to each location but often returned several times. It was more than the husbands could take.

"Let's go look at shoes Ben."

"Yeah. Anything would be better than this."

Both men browsed through the men's shoe department until something caught Bud's eye.

"Look at those cowboy boots. I've always wanted a pair. They say they're comfortable... Bloody expensive though."

"I can't imagine why you'd go to Hawaii to buy cowboy boots. But who am I to say? Why don't you try them on?"

"Why not?"

Bud looked at a pair of fancy alligator skin boots which appealed to him. He liked their shiny smoothness and rich textured appearance. They had that 'urban cowboy' appeal he considered to be the 'in' look. He picked up a pair and checked the size.

Size ten – perfect!

The next step was to find a chair in order to try them on. He knew they would look good on him. But their expensive price caused him to pause in thought.

Why shouldn't he splurge? Tina was always buying everything in the world to give away to relatives when they returned from trips. It didn't matter whether it was a major one like this or just a weekend getaway.

She bought presents for everyone else but them. That really annoyed him since it added considerably to the holiday's cost. Here was an example of something he had always wanted for himself but never bought. Damn it! This time he would take the plunge.

"How're you making out Bud? Your face is all red."

"Shit. I can't get this boot on. It's tighter than you are when Janice makes long distance phone calls."

"Keep trying. They're supposed to soften up as soon as you get them on."

"Eeee...rrrrrrrrr...gggggrrh! There! The little buggar is on! But my heel is up to my asshole. I think I'm going to be lame for life."

"Try walking."

"I'm lame I told you! I can't even hobble with this bloody boot on!" Bud knew he wasn't going to get the other boot on. His instep throbbed with pain and his foot felt like it was in a vice. "The hell with it. I'm taking this thing off." He stretched and twisted and pulled and cursed. The boot remained glued to his foot. "I can't get the damn thing to budge! Ben give me a hand will you?"

Ben grabbed hold of the boot with both hands and yanked hard pulling Bud right out of the chair. He landed in a heap on top of Ben. The boot remained intact. It was time to call for the manager.

"Hey where the hell is the manager? This boot's glued to my foot and won't let go. I want the bloody thing off. **NOW! ... RIGHT NOW!"**

At the sound of Bud's yelling, the manager rushed over from the other side of the department.

"Yes sir. Is there a problem?"

"Is there a problem? What kind of a dumb question is that? As you can see I can't get this goddamn boot off. **See!** My buddy here can't get it off either."

"Is the other gentleman stuck in a boot as well?"

"No you smart ass! He can't get **MY** boot off. Now what are you going to do about it?"

"Settle down and we'll try to pull it off."

Bud sat back and offered his foot to the manager who began pulling. He pulled, first facing one direction and then pulled again, facing the opposite direction. It was useless! The man lacked the strength that Ben had shown when he yanked Bud from the chair. No way was he going to get the boot off with this namby pamby approach.

"Hey Bud, if we can't get that one off we should at least put the other one on so your feet match," Ben taunted.

"Buggar off!"

Now Bud was hobbling around the shoe department. The manager had given up. On one foot he wore a magnificent looking alligator skin cowboy boot and on the other a beat up old sneaker. The contrast was hilarious, made even more so by the pained look on Bud's face. Ben started to laugh.

"Ha ha ha! Oh God, this is a sight! Imagine, Bud flunks boot camp. Ha ha!"

Once again Bud confronted the manager.

"Ignore that stupid hyena over there. What are you going to do about this boot?"

"Can I give you a deal?"

"Never mind the dumb jokes! Get this thing off and right now!"

"We'll have to cut it off. Hang on while I get a knife."

The manager returned with a knife and proceeded to cut the boot off Bud's foot. At $175 a pair what a waste!

"Ben let's get out of here and grab a drink until the women are ready to leave." Bud's instep was still smarting as he limped beside side Ben on the way to a nearby bar.

After two or three drinks the men felt mellower and grew more tolerant of the shopping trip. They began taking good natured shots at each other.

"Boy did you look funny trying to take off that boot. You should have seen your face as you got more and more pissed off."

"Some help you were. For a tugboat skipper you couldn't navigate your way through the shoe department. As Janice would say why don't you 'toot off'?"

"Then why don't you 'boot off'?" quipped Ben, pleased with his play on words.

"Wait till you're older and in your wheelchair – I'll run you over."

"Yeah well you'll be in your wheelchair at that time too."

Just then the women burst into the room. Tina was first, her arms laden with purchases. Janice hobbled painfully behind taking slow, carefully placed steps.

"There you are! We had no trouble finding you two. The nearest bar always does it. Come on Janice we may as well join these two alkies for a drink."

"What's with you Janice? You're walking like Bud does when he wears cowboy boots," Ben queried.

"It's these bloody thongs. I'm a walking-wounded with blisters on my toes."

"You should have seen Bud perform back in the store. He was walking just like you."

"Piss off Ben! They don't need to know everything."

The women sat down at the table and placed their orders. Janice ordered a Mai Tai and Tina a dry red wine with ice on the side. When the drinks arrived they reached for them with great eagerness. It had been a grueling day and the ladies looked forward to a drink and some relaxation before returning to Waikiki for the last night of their holiday.

For once the Whites were not returning to Seattle after the Toppers. This time Ben had to adjust his schedule for business purposes and as a result he and Janice booked the same flight.

Suddenly an ear shattering noise erupted in the room.

"Shit! Goddamn shit!"

The scream shattered the stillness of the bar as patrons craned their necks to see the cause of the sudden commotion.

"Why do these things always happen to me?**"** Tina demanded as she cringed from the table. **"Look! There it is! There it is!"**

Janice joined Tina in a sudden departure from the table while Bud and Ben sat with exasperated expressions on their faces.

"It's just a cockroach. My God you're in the tropics. What do you expect?"

"I don't care. I want to get out of this filthy place. Take me to the Melting Pot."

Bud shrugged at the bartender as he paid the tab. What could he say? He was surprised that Tina had never seen a cockroach in the Melting Pot since they were sure as hell around.

They hailed a cab and returned to Waikiki. It was agreed to meet at the Melting Pot in two hours to begin spending their last evening before departure.

Tina and Bud arrived at the pub on time. It would be another three hours before the Whites would finally appear.

* * * * *

After returning to their apartment, Ben and Janice decided to take a nap before proceeding to the Melting Pot. They closed all of the drapes and fell asleep in the pitch black darkness of their bed room.

"Ring! ... RRRR...iii...nn ...g!"

From somewhere in the darkness Ben heard the sound of the telephone. He turned over and pulled the covers over his head, hoping the sound would go away. It wouldn't. The sound continued unabated as he turned first to the left and then to the right. "Who in hell is calling?" he muttered to himself as he shook the cobwebs from his head and reached over to the receiver on the night stand.

"**Ben!**" Rocco pleaded, "**Get over here right away. I'm in the alley behind the Sailor's Bar in Honolulu. Hurry!**"

Suddenly the phone went dead.

He yanked on his pants, zippered his fly and pulled his t-shirt over his head. Next Ben shuffled his way into his sneakers and headed toward the door.

"Where're you going? Janice demanded. "We're supposed to go to the Melting Pot in an hour."

"Rocco's in trouble. I'm going over to Honolulu," he replied as he rushed out the door.

It took Ben awhile to find someone who would lend him a car. By that time dusk had fallen and cloud cover added to the darkness of the evening. Finally he made a contact and shortly after arrived at the Sailor's Bar. It was a seedy joint with a reputation for fights and drug deals. He proceeded around the building to the back alley and down the passageway – it was gloomy with no sign of life. There was something sinister about his surroundings, making the hair on the back of his neck stand up. Suddenly he caught a slight movement in his peripheral vision. He spun around to meet the object head on, ready to either defend himself or run like hell.

"**Shit!**" he muttered through clenched teeth. "It's just a cat."

He continued down the alleyway – all senses on alert. There was no moon tonight and the stars were obscured by the haze, creating an eerie darkness. Suddenly he stumbled over an object on the ground and fell head first to the pavement.

Damn, he thought, *who the hell would just leave something in the middle of the alley?*

Looking more closely the object began to take form in the pitch darkness. "**My God! It's a body!**" Ben cried aloud. He made out its ashen white face and blood covered torso. As shocking as that was, he suddenly stiffened as recognition took hold. "**Holy shit! It's Rocco!**"

Ben panicked. He beat a hasty retreat, jumped in the car and dug out, heading recklessly for Waikiki.

He arrived, breathless, back to the condo and filled Janice in. "**Rocco's dead and his body is covered with blood!**" Ben blurted out.

"Get a hold of yourself," Janice responded. "We can't do anything about it. Let's go and see Bud and Tina."

"Where the hell have you guys been?" Bud accused when they arrived at the table.

Bud's greeting was met with a stony silence. Janice sat there with a blank expression on her face and Ben was noticeably upset.

"What's wrong?" Tina asked.

"Rocco was found dead! Ben found him covered in blood in an alley," Janice responded. "It's likely he was stabbed to death by someone who was an expert in using a knife."

"My God!" Tina responded. It was a shock to hear of the murder with such stark abruptness. But she and Bud had expected something of this nature to happen sooner or later in view of Rocco's rumored underground connections.

The word quickly got around the room and a sadness infiltrated the bar. One of the family had died and this was cause for the regulars to go into mourning. Rita the barmaid seemed most upset. Mia, on the other hand, didn't appear shaken at all. The Admiral, wearing a smirk on his face, tried to lighten everyone up. Brad, the accountant from Chicago, just sat there with no expression at all. It wasn't clear whether he was drunk or had just withdrawn into his shell, oblivious to the rest of the world.

"Let's go! It's too sad in here. Rick will cheer us up," Tina suggested.

The party shuffled out of their chairs and prepared to leave.

On the way to the club Ben spoke of the numerous calls for aid he had received from Rocco and how frustrating it had been, not knowing where he was so he could help.

Walking along Kalakaua Avenue they passed several prostitutes. Some were standing at the ready in an attempt to catch the eyes of males walking along the street either with or without female companions.

Others were engaged in an active game of pursuit chasing Asian males down the street and into any buildings they entered for sanctuary.

The two couples finally arrived at the club just as the second set was about to start. The band members nodded knowingly in their direction as the party of four shuffled toward an empty table.

"Welcome to the Rick Stevens show!" one of the sidemen announced. "Here he is ladies and gentlemen. Put your hands together for the one and only Rick Stevens!"

Rick rushed through the audience and leapt onto the stage. At that instant his band hit the first note and he launched into *New York, New York*. Part way through the song he noticed the foursome and winked at them as he kicked up his heels during his choreographed version of the song. During his first break Rick dropped by the table to say hello. He knew it was their last night and hoped to cheer them up.

"Hi y 'all. How you all doing? Having a good time?"

"We're a bit down in the dumps, not only is it our last night we've just found out that Rocco was murdered."

"Really! I never knew him very well but heard he worked for The Man. Did you know the rumor is that The Man drinks at the pub you guys frequent? I don't know who he is but The Man has a reputation for being ruthless. Wouldn't it be ironic if The Man was really a woman? Just a thought. Well I'm due for the next set. See y'all later."

Rick returned to the stage and began his second set. Using two or three songs to gradually build up the tempo – then to the audience's delight he launched into *Shout*.

"Now let's move to something a little quieter for my friends over there from Seattle. It's their last night in Waikiki this evening and I want to do this song especially for them." Rick then sang the beautiful, but sad, words of *Honolulu City Lights*.

A nostalgic mood gripped each of them as fond memories of Honolulu mingled with sad thoughts of departure. After the song was over the group waved goodbye to Rick and left the club.

Chapter 12

The Return Home

A bittersweet sadness lingered in the room as the Toppers packed their bags in preparation for the return home. On one hand it would be nice to get back to see other friends and relatives, but on the other hand the holiday had passed far too quickly and it would be another year before their next visit. Tina was busy folding garments neatly and gingerly, placing each of them in a predetermined location in the suitcases. She seemed to take forever as Bud impatiently paced the floor.

"Hurry up!" Bud demanded. "We'll be late for the cab that Ben and Janice are coming in. Hell if I was packing I'd throw those clothes into the bags in two minutes. You'll end up ironing them again when we get home anyway."

"Go to hell!" came the reply.

"Why do we have to carry all of those damn plastic bags separately when they can be jammed into the suitcases?"

Half a dozen plastic bags containing shoes, macadamia nuts and chocolates were strewn over the bed.

"I'm taking the first load down on the elevator," Bud announced as he struggled through the doorway and out into the hallway. *What a pain in the ass*! he thought as he carried assorted bags, suitcases and articles of clothing onto the elevator. Although it took forever to reach the ground floor Bud didn't mind. He had cursed the slowness of the elevator earlier in the holiday but now he wanted the trip to linger.

On Bud's return to the apartment, after depositing the items from the first trip in the lobby, the telephone began to ring. Tina lunged at it.

"Yeah? What d'ya want? This is Tina and Bud's pizza joint. How'd you like your order? We have a wide selection of Topper's toppings." She was ready to continue with the charade sure that Janice was on the other end.

"Is this, or is it not, the Topper residence?" interrupted a reserved voice at the other end.

"Why yes it is."

"Well my dear lady this is Mr. Rollins calling. I'd like to talk to Mr. Topper if you don't mind."

"One moment please!" Tina screwed up her nose as she handed the phone to Bud.

"Yes this is Bud Topper. Of course Mr. Rollins we'll be there shortly to pick it up and I look forward to meeting you." Bud glared at Tina. "Dammit! Of all the times for you to fool around on the phone. That was Mr. Rollins, a very important client of our firm, and he's more straight laced than a jock strap on a missionary."

"Well, the hell with him then! It's time he loosened up and enjoyed life."

There was no point in arguing further so Bud began his second trip on the elevator. When the door opened at ground level hoards of people with luggage and assorted bags and boxes, jammed their way onto the elevator. Bud looked at them enviously in spite of the pasty white complexions they wore. They were brand new arrivals who, at their vacation's end, would repeat the same ritual he was currently undertaking.

Ben's face suddenly appeared around the corner. "Are y'all ready? I got a deal on our trip out to the airport but we can't keep him waiting."

As soon as Bud saw the car he grew very irritated. "I thought you were going to book a regular cab. This piece of junk is worse than the one we arrived in three weeks ago."

"My buddy here needs the money and he'll charge us less than a cab."

The car was a disgrace! Rust permeated all parts of the body and dents were everywhere. It was a four-color job: most of it was yellow, one door was blue, the hood was covered with grey primer paint and the balance of the body was covered in an orange brown rust. Inside the vehicle the upholstery was stained and torn in a number of places. Springs protruded from the back seat. What a beauty! Right out of the showcase at the local junkyard.

Janice stood away from the car trying not to be linked to it in any way. Ben, on the other hand, didn't give a damn as he leaned against the hood and winked at the women who passed by. The driver remained stone-faced in his seat oblivious to any reaction to his car. He was anxious to pick up the party and be on his way.

"We have another trip to make in the elevator. Tina is still doing some packing and we haven't given away our leftover foodstuffs, cleaning supplies and booze yet."

"Give your leftover stuff to our driver Joe here. It's part of the deal I made," Ben shouted after Bud as he headed for the elevator.

On the way out to the airport Bud had to stop to pick up the important papers Mr. Rollins phoned about. A couple of days ago Bud's boss had called to tell him that Mr. Ron Rollins, president of Rynot Funding Incorporated, was holidaying at an exclusive condominium complex on the outskirts of Waikiki and to expect a call. Bud was to pick up confidential documents that dealt with the merger of two large corporations. The phone call from Mr. Rollins was a reminder of the errand's importance.

Bud had never met Mr. Rollins before but had heard plenty about him. Rollins was a multi-millionaire, a self made man driven to succeed in business at all costs. He worked sixteen hour days, seven days a week and never took a holiday unless it related to business. His expectations of employees and business associates were also demanding. If they didn't measure up to his standards they were given their walking papers. His standards not only included honesty, effectiveness in and dedication toward the job, but also clean living, good social graces and smartness in dress and deportment.

"Christ," Bud thought. "What is Rollins going to think when we roll up in this junk pile? I never should have let Ben make the transportation arrangements."

Eventually they got underway. The car backfired a couple of times before the driver jerked his way out of the driveway of the hotel. Some of the suitcases protruded from the trunk which was lashed down by rope while other luggage and boxes were tied on top. The car and its contents drew the attention of the occupants of several other cars as it spun its way down the street. Adding to the spectacle was the burly driver himself who must have weighed over three hundred pounds. He had long bushy hair, wore torn and dirty clothing and had grown a bushy unkempt beard.

Bud settled into the soiled and torn upholstery in the back seat. He wanted to sink out of sight and to pretend Ben hadn't arranged this circus, but he couldn't and there was a very important stop on the way.

"Hey pal we have to stop at 1221 Alu Way before we go to the airport," Bud called out to the driver.

"Awright! That's a ritzy joint ya know. They never let me in there b'fore – I tried t'go couple times. Guess ah don' know the right people."

"What kind of a joint are you taking us to Bud? I hate going to snooty places," Tina responded.

"I have to pick up a parcel from a very important client of my company's. Be sure you're all on your best behavior. God I wish we were in a respectable taxi cab!"

"Oh don't be such a snob. We'll make a real good impression. Right Janice?"

"Right. The only riff raff here are Ben and Bud."

The multi-colored junker turned the corner and rolled up to the gatehouse guarding access to the complex. The driver stopped and an officious looking guard glared at them through the window.

"And what d'ya want? This piece of junk isn't allowed in here."

"Up your nose!" Janice responded. "We're here to see a very important person."

"Oh yeah! Who?"

"What's his name Bud? That nerd you were telling us about?"

"Rollins. Mr. Rollins."

"Just a minute til I call him. What's yer name?"

"Mr. Topper of Puget Mutual and I'm here to pick up a parcel from Mr. Rollins."

"Okay go head. First time a junkpile's going ta foul the streets o' the complex though."

"You're an asshole aren't you!" Ben shouted as he waved a clenched fist at the uniformed guard.

The car travelled straight ahead for two blocks and then turned right before stopping in front of an executive style townhouse. A man was standing on the sidewalk in front of the building. He wore a neatly pressed pair of beige slacks, polished brogues, and a silk shirt with a scarf folded round his neck and through to the opening at the front of his shirt. He carried a Gucci bag in his left hand and a brown envelope in his right.

"There he is! It must be him. Look at the expensive looking rings on his fingers. The guy must be loaded for such a nerd!" Tina cried out.

Her voice was loud enough for the figure on the sidewalk to hear.

"Hi there Mr. Rollins. I'm Tina Topper. I recognize you from your voice on the phone. Wanna buy a pizza?"

"My God!" Bud muttered under his breath. "What a way to make a first impression!"

* * * * *

They finally arrived at the airport later than planned and ran in to wall-to-wall people lining the departure area. The queue to the check-in counter was horrendous. It was likely they would get a poor seating arrangement for the return trip to Seattle.

"Ben," Janice suggested, "Why don't you put on your special hat and get us to the front of this line?"

"It won't work in this line-up since places have already been established."

"Well do something! I want a window seat in the smoking area."

"I'll try."

Ben promptly disappeared from sight, leaving them standing in line with the luggage. He headed toward the bank of payphones located on the floor above the throng. From that vantage point he still had a view of the check-in counter. He dropped a coin in the slot and dialed the number of the airline reservation counter.

"Hello, Western Airlines reservations? I have reservations for Seattle on Flight one hundred and twelve. I would like to reserve four seats in the smoking section. Four across beginning with a window."

"I'm sorry sir. We can't reserve seats in advance except in special circumstances."

"This is a special circumstance. We're caught in a traffic jam and I'm calling on my cellular phone in my limousine."

"Sorry sir."

"But we'll miss our flight. My wife needs a window seat or she'll make a scene at the airport."

"I said I'm sorry! What makes you think you should get special treatment?"

"Not as sorry as I'm going to be when I tell Janice and Tina."

Ben knew he had struck out and did not hide his annoyance with the voice at the other end of the line. He suddenly had an urge to get back at her.

"Hey! You don't know where I am do you?"

"No I don't know where you are and I couldn't care less. Should I?"

"Sure you should. Look up over your left shoulder to the level above you where the telephones are."

She looked in the direction Ben had described, scanning the area in an attempt to find him. Eventually she found him. A shocked look crept over her face. Staring back at her was Ben's bum. His pants were down and he was bent forward with his rear end facing her.

"Up yours!" he gestured. Mooning gave him a measure of satisfaction and reminded him of his college days. Next he beat a hasty retreat.

All of a sudden a hand with a vice-like grip seized him by the shoulder and spun him around. Opposite stood a heavy set man with a pronounced 5-o'clock shadow.

"Hey Mac you Ben White?" he growled.

"Oh my God!" Ben groaned. "They're going to pinch me for mooning in the airport and they already know my name."

"I asked ya Mac, are ya Ben White? I'm with the Hawaiian Police Department!" He flashed his badge.

"**Yes officer that's him. I told you before. I know it's him!**" screamed a voice from somewhere in the midst of the crowd which had gathered by this time.

"**Let HIM answer, lady!**"

"I told ya it was him, didn't I? You calling me a liar?"

"Listen lady, shut up while I handle this."

"Don't tell me t' shut up, ya dumb dick. It was 'cause of me ya even knew where t' look for him."

That voice – it sounded familiar. Who was it? He peered into the crowd and there she was. It was Pam the eccentric old lady from the beach. By this time Ben realized he wasn't going to be pinched for exposing himself. It must be something else.

"What's the problem officer?" he asked, momentarily relieved.

"Where were you yest'day?"

"At the shopping mall with friends. There were four of us, why?"

"You know a guy named Rocco?"

"Yes."

"Come with me over to the detention room."

"But I'll miss my plane. It leaves for Seattle in half an hour."

"It won't take long. That is if I get the right answers. Over this way."

The rest of Ben's party had checked in and received their seats by this time. However due to their late arrival each couple was assigned seats in a different part of the plane. It would be a long trip back, Bud thought, with no opportunity for conversation among the four of them to help pass the time.

"Where's Ben?" Janice asked out loud. "We're going to leave shortly and he hasn't come back."

"There he is over there walking into that room with that fat man!" Tina responded. "Hey isn't that Pam from the beach lurking behind them?"

"Yeah I think it is," Bud added. "She's prob'ly here on the lookout for some stud."

"Don't be ridiculous. She hates all of you guys."

"Flight one hundred and twelve to Seattle is now ready for pre-boarding through gate nine," the announcement blared through the public address system.

"I better get Ben!" Janice cried in a panic.

"Okay Janice. Hurry! We'll be getting on soon."

Janice disappeared into the crowd heading in the direction of the doorway of the room that Ben and the fat man disappeared into. A knot formed in the pit of her stomach as she worried they may miss the flight.

Several minutes later the announcement was made to board all other passengers. There was still no sign of Ben or Janice.

"That bloody Ben," Bud exclaimed. "He'll do anything to return home after us. He prob'ly staged all of this so he could wave at us as we go back to Seattle."

"He wouldn't do that. Their bags are all checked in and Janice knew nothing about it."

"Well I wouldn't put it past him."

By this time all the passengers were seated and the flight attendants were getting ready to demonstrate safety precautions. Ben and Janice were still not on the plane. It was likely they would miss it.

"I'm worried about them Bud."

"Why? I told you earlier that Ben prob'ly had this set up all along so he could spend more time than us at the beach."

An attendant was about to close the boarding door when a commotion could be heard from the vicinity of the loading ramp.

"Hold it! Hold it dammit! We're on this plane!" It was Ben's voice.

Tina heaved a sigh of relief when she recognized it.

Ben's head appeared through the doorway first, closely followed by Janice's. Tina and Bud were both dying of curiosity as the plane was readied for take off. It wouldn't be until after the plane reached cruising altitude that they could move up the aisle to where the other two sat in order to find out what happened.

As soon as the seatbelt sign went off Tina sprung from her seat. Bud followed close behind.

"What happened? What happened?" Tina demanded as soon as she reached them.

"Oh nothing," Ben replied. "We were just visiting with your good friend Pam."

"Come on. I know Pam was at the airport. We saw her. But what really happened? I'm dying to know."

"Nothing."

"Oh go ahead and tell them Ben," Janice directed.

"That fat old broad sicked the police on me that's what happened."

"What do you mean?"

"Well the police were around the beach asking questions about Rocco's murder and she was more than pleased to tell them I hung around with him. She even told them I was probably escaping through the airport at that very minute. So she just hopped in the cop car and got a free ride to the airport with lights flashing and sirens blaring. She offered to point me out since they didn't know what I looked like. I think she just wanted the attention."

"So what happened when he questioned you?"

"He asked a lot of questions. But after I told him all four of us were at the shopping mall when the murder was committed he said I could go. He took my Seattle address though."

"You know Tina, I'm annoyed with her too." Janice piped in. "She claims to be our friend but hates both Ben and Bud."

"Yeah!" the men chimed in unison.

"In fact she prob'ly killed Rocco herself," Bud offered.

As views of the city and Diamond Head faded in the distance they settled into the routine of the flight. Each of them reflected on recent events. It was a shock that Rocco was murdered and that Pam had tried to implicate Ben. Who had done it? Was it The Man? Who was The Man? Rick said he drank at the pub. Did they know him? Could it have been Brad? The Admiral? Rick? Or even Mia or Pam? Was The Man a woman?

These questions ran over and over through their minds – tormenting their thoughts during the long trip home.

No answer was forthcoming.